ON THE CALCULATION
OF VOLUME

ON THE CALCULATION OF VOLUME

BOOK IV

SOLVEJ BALLE

Translated from the Danish by
Sophia Hersi Smith and Jennifer Russell

faber

First published in 2026
by Faber & Faber Ltd
The Bindery, 51 Hatton Garden
London EC1N 8HN

First published in Danish in 2022 under the title
Om udregning af rumfang IV by Pelagraf, Denmark

Typeset by Faber & Faber Ltd
Printed in the UK by CPI Group (UK) Ltd, Croydon CR0 4YY

All rights reserved
© Solvej Balle, 2022
Translation © Sophia Hersi Smith and Jennifer Russell, 2026

The translators would like to thank Barbara J. Haveland
for her keen eye and generous guidance.

The right of Solvej Balle to be identified as author of this work
has been asserted in accordance with Section 77 of the Copyright,
Designs and Patents Act 1988

*This is a work of fiction. All of the characters, organisations
and events portrayed in this novel are either products of the author's
imagination or are used fictitiously*

A CIP record for this book
is available from the British Library

ISBN 978–0–571–39703–7

Printed and bound in the UK on FSC® certified paper in line with our continuing
commitment to ethical business practices, sustainability and the environment.
For further information see faber.co.uk/environmental-policy

Our authorised representative in the EU for product safety is
Easy Access System Europe, Mustamäe tee 50, 10621 Tallinn, Estonia
gpsr.requests@easproject.com

2 4 6 8 10 9 7 5 3 1

ON THE CALCULATION OF VOLUME

1892

It is hard to know where something ends and where something begins. Or someone. Where a person starts or stops. Where the next begins. You think you can see it: the bodies with air in between. Five people at a gate that swung open. They had rung the intercom at our wrought-iron gate and now they stood there, waiting. Somewhat spread out, but a group nonetheless.

They must have seen the same thing we did when we came walking down from the house: a group of sorts. Four people with air in between making their way to the gate, and now we are nine people in a house. Nine people who met at the gate, and who remember that we met at the gate. That we came walking, almost running, down to them and that they stood there, hesitating, if you can call it hesitation when you've already pressed the buzzer: Anton Janas in a grey wool overcoat with chunky buttons; Rosalie Torpa, who prefers to go by Rosi – stress on the second syllable; Sonia Mirbek, who had pressed the buzzer and then moved back a bit towards Peter Hass-Teilo, who stood a few steps from the gate and laid his hand on Sonia's shoulder when it began to open.

It did so because Ralf had pressed the button in the house upon hearing the insistent ringing. We had been in the hall, stacking cardboard boxes of provisions when the buzzer went. Ralf, who was nearest to it, gave a start but then opened the door, stepped outside and peered down at the gate. At first all he could see were a few figures and part of a car. He could not see how many there were, but he could see that they were standing there, so he pressed the button to let them in and we hurried down the driveway. First Ralf, then Henry and lastly Olga and me.

It took only a few moments for us to grasp that the new arrivals were looking for someone called Ralf, and that they were caught in the eighteenth of November. We invited them in and shortly after we were all gathered in the house. We had managed to manoeuvre the car through the gate. It was Peter who drove, and Ralf who guided him to the spot in front of the old garage. I don't remember exactly where Marlice Maurer had positioned herself in the group. She must have been behind one of the others because I didn't really notice her until we were up at the house. By then, the gate had long since swung shut behind them, the car had been parked in front of the garage, people were edging their way past all the cardboard boxes piled high in the hall and soon we were standing around chatting about porridge oats, because that's what was in the boxes: oats and salted oregano crackers.

Marlice was the last to enter the house, having bent down to tie her shoelaces before she too stepped into the hall. For a moment, she paused, eyeing the stairs to the first floor and glancing into the rooms on either side. She wiped her feet on the mat and sidled past the boxes, but after only a few moments she insisted on taking off her shoes. This was just after she had noticed the floor in the largest of the living rooms: the patterns and inlays in different woods. Typical of houses of that period, she said shortly after, when we were standing in the middle of the room – in our stockinged feet, because I too had taken off my shoes, out of consideration for the floors, I suppose – but she didn't have a chance to say much more about the period before the others came flocking in, asking for a tour. I think they were surprised by the size of the place, even though they had seen it from the outside, and maybe we were also surprised by the sudden commotion in the house: a flurry of people, of feet being wiped on the mat, of jackets and scarves being hung on hooks in the hall, of voices and sentences filling the air, questions about the house and how many we are and how long we have lived here. One person wants to know where the bathroom is, another almost trips over a pair of shoes or a cardboard box, someone else moves a couple of boxes to the side and makes some remark about the house and suddenly you cannot tell whose shoes are whose or whose sentence you have ringing in your ears.

We showed them around, and we knew: that they would be moving in. It was hard to imagine anything other than them coming to live here. There is plenty of room, and now they've gone into town to collect their things since we stayed up so late last night, talking into the early hours, that they never got round to doing it then. We were either too tired or had drunk too much wine to drive anywhere.

By the time the newcomers had finished their tour of the ground floor and the rooms upstairs, Olga had made tea and fetched some crackers from one of the boxes, and we all gathered in the drawing room with its big open fireplace. They could see the basement any time, she said, as we settled into the old sofas and armchairs, sitting closer together than usual, because we were used to sprawling on our furniture, legs up and blankets wrapped around us, since it can get a bit chilly if we don't light a fire.

But now Ralf did light a fire and we sat there in the drawing room. With names and explanations swirling in the air around us. With a welter of words, with gesticulations and stories: Sonia and Peter on one sofa with Ralf, and Olga on a cushion by the fire, from which she occasionally tossed another log onto the embers. Now and then she would lean forward and blow on the fire if it was taking too long to catch.

I sat on the floor next to Olga until it became too warm in front of the fire, then I moved up onto the other sofa next to Henry. The others lounged in the armchairs, or at least for the most part they did, because Rosi and Marlice in particular moved around quite a bit, standing in the doorway, where it was slightly cooler, or tagging along with one of the residents of the house when they left the room – to get more crackers or make tea or bring up wine from the cellar – but these were no more than brief intermissions and before long we would all be back in the drawing room, where more and more pieces of our shared story were laid out. A room full of movement: time rushed by in our retellings, streams of eighteenths of November, we sped through our days and soon it was evening and there we were, nine people in the drawing room with voices and sentences, with everything that had happened, all our solitary beginnings and, later, our encounters.

To begin with we were two groups: ourselves and our guests, or the newcomers and the residents of the house, but at some point, I'm not sure when, the newcomers stopped being our guests and became the newest residents of the house. Possibly after just a couple of hours. In any case, late into the night, by the time we brought out mattresses and blankets and quilts, they no longer felt like guests. Or at least, I think it reminded us that we ourselves were guests, that these were the house's mattresses and the house's sofas we were offering them to sleep on, that they were not really ours. Perhaps that's how it is: we are guests, and when we have guests, it reminds us that everything is on loan, that we've been sitting on borrowed sofas and chairs, with arms and legs that are ours, belonging to bodies that are ours, and all the words and sentences, all the gestures, none of which are truly our own. That much was clear to us, since we couldn't help but borrow one another's gestures. Or sentences.

It is easy enough to tell them apart. The bodies on the sofas and armchairs. The faces belonging to the bodies. The voices belonging to the faces. You listen first to one, then to another, and each time you turn your gaze towards one of the voices, you find that it belongs to a face and to a body with a hand behind its head or a way of leaning on the arm of the sofa. But then you realise that you have a hand behind your own head or that you are leaning in exactly the same way, and then someone else is telling a story and someone else again is borrowing a gesture. A leg is bent and drawn up onto a sofa, a pair of hands flits about, illustrating a point, and moments later another pair of hands flits and another leg is drawn up onto an armchair. It is warm in the room and someone picks up a sentence and repurposes it, because even though you quickly learn to recognise the voices and match them to faces and bodies, their movements ripple through the group, sentences are passed along and gestures are mimicked or echoed, sometimes it's just the twitch of an eyebrow or the tilt of a head travelling quietly from one person to the next. Someone gets up to collect cups or glasses and another immediately does the same, and that was how the evening was spent: a mosaic, a mishmash, so many gestures and all these hands and arms and legs borrowing and copying and mirroring and reciprocating. One person yawns, then another, and then a third, because everyone is tired, but that doesn't stop us. One story is sent out into the room and then another follows, because someone has a similar experience to latch onto it: one person's account elicits a memory from another and suddenly you see something that's happened or somewhere you've been in a whole new light. Borrowed plumage, stolen mannerisms, a way of resting a cheek in a hand, a benign theft: Rosi holding her teacup in both hands, staring into space, and then there's Olga in the same pose. That is how the first evening went, with us weaving into one another, in a chain dance, a strange ballet, a clumsy pantomime.

It got to be very late. Our attention seemed to be running out. Most of us were sleepy or had drunk too much wine. First Rosi dozed off, then Olga felt the urge to go on one of her walks in the dark. The rest of us carried on talking for a little while longer, but our movements had slowed. Sonia leaned against Peter, and Henry stretched a bit, as if he too would have liked to lean against someone. The conversation petered out and did not resume until Olga returned from her nocturnal stroll.

Olga was now wide awake, we heard her bustling about in the kitchen, organising beds for our guests. She had dug out the old mattresses stowed away in one of the rooms behind the kitchen, and when she dragged out the first of these and let it drop with a thud in one of the adjoining rooms, we all got up to assist her. Rosi rather more slowly as she had to wake up first, but soon everyone was busy pushing mattresses from room to room and rustling up blankets and extra quilts, and last of all Olga produced her old sleeping bag, which still – or so she claimed – smelled of salt water and the Frisian Islands.

I said they might not get much sleep on those hard mattresses. That we could get hold of others later, but everyone was tired, or almost everyone, I think. It took me a couple of hours to fall asleep, and this morning I was the first to wake, or at least I think I was, because all was quiet when I crept down the stairs. Maybe they were just pretending to be asleep. In any case, it wasn't until I had made coffee, fetched porridge oats from the boxes in the hall and set out cups and plates on the table in the conservatory that they began to surface from mattresses and sofas. And there we sat. There was room for everyone around the table and everyone remembered what had happened: that five people had stood outside a gate which had swung open and that four people had come walking, almost running, down to the gate.

After breakfast I retreated to my room, thinking that I might be able to sleep a little more, but my head is buzzing: with people and gestures and five new intertwining stories that have been there all along, even though we did not know it.

It feels as though we had each been walking along our own path in the same forest. As though we had got lost and had done so separately, but we were not alone in being lost, because the others were on the paths too. And now we have found our way to a clearing and suddenly we see that we share not only the clearing but the forest too. We think it begins when we meet, but in fact our stories were already entwined.

The others have gone into town, I heard both cars drive off, our new housemates have gone to collect their things and Ralf and Henry have driven to Ralf's flat to pick up more plates and some pots and pans that Ralf remembered he had stored in his attic.

I think Olga is awake. She did not come down for breakfast and I have just heard footsteps in the hallway. Maybe the others have returned, but I don't think so. Now I hear it again, and there is just one person. It is the sound of someone walking barefoot.

1895

Naturally we assumed that they had known each other for a long time when they appeared in front of our wrought-iron gate, but they hadn't. That is to say, Marlice and Rosi had. They met in a park in Amsterdam after only a couple of hundred days. Day # 236, said Marlice last night as we sat in the drawing room once again, sharing all our days with one another. They had met while the rest of us were still wandering about, believing we were alone.

They met Anton Janas much later, in Poland. And after they met him, all three had travelled to Berlin. That was where they had seen one of our posters. That was why they had come here. Not immediately – it took some time for them to realise that something was amiss, even after seeing the poster. It read *Ralf Kern* and *the eighteenth of November* in large letters. It read *Bremen* and *Henselstraße*. They had noticed the somewhat cryptic wording and the large type, but otherwise it was just a poster, and only after seeing several other notices about the same Ralf Kern at the station's ticket office did they start to wonder. Not so much because someone was missing – it was just a single sheet of paper with a photograph, a short text and a couple of phone numbers – but because the notice had moved around from day to day, irregularly, as if there had been a change in the days. One day Anton had seen a notice on a glass wall near the ticket office, but a few days later he and Rosi had walked past a similar notice reading *the eighteenth of November* and *missing* and *Ralf Kern*, this time posted on a pillar a little further off. Rosi remarked that she had seen the same notice in a completely different spot, and they talked about the poster that had long been hanging on a wall alongside advertisements for concerts, exhibitions and events. It had to be the same Ralf K. who was missing. The next time Rosi passed a notice, now posted once again on the glass wall by the ticket office, she took it down, folded it and put it in her pocket, and there it had stayed until it disappeared on its own, probably that same night; in any case, when she thought of it again it was gone, and they had put off their questions until later. It didn't seem all that remarkable that a man had gone missing on precisely the eighteenth of November, Marlice said to Ralf, as if to justify why they hadn't set out in search of him right away. She was, I think, the one who found the missing Ralf Kern least remarkable. To begin with, at any rate.

It was only later, when the topic of the strange notices came up again, that they decided to do something about the matter, but by then no more missing-person notices were appearing at the ticket office, and when they enquired at first one ticket counter, then another, no one knew anything about them. The man must have been found, Rosi had said, but then it dawned on her that this was impossible. If the man was gone on the morning of the eighteenth, he had to be gone again with the arrival of the next eighteenth. Even if he had been found during the day. Unless something was not right.

Of course, they had suspected that something was wrong – which is to say that both this man and those searching for him had to be stuck in the eighteenth just as they were. But now, when they finally began to investigate, only the large poster remained, still affixed to the wall where Henry had hung it on his trip to Berlin.

The three had started to consider whether they should go to Bremen and look for Ralf when Anton suddenly spotted another poster at the opposite end of the station, and he was convinced someone must have put it up recently. It had, of course, been there all along – at least, Henry was certain that he'd put up two posters at the station in Berlin. Anton must have overlooked one the first time, though he found that unlikely.

Either way, the mystery of the posters and the disappearing missing-person notices only made this Ralf K. all the more intriguing. But now nothing was happening at all. Two posters, no change, no explanation. All three of them had become more and more convinced that there must be others in the eighteenth of November, but now their search for the mysterious Ralf K. felt like being on the lookout for a mythical creature, as if they were hunting a sea monster, or Father Christmas or the Abominable Snowman, said Anton. And in the days that followed, they often stopped by Berlin Hauptbahnhof just to confirm that nothing had changed this time either. In the end, they had come to Bremen with no other clues to go by than Henselstraße and Ralf's name.

We were again sitting around the fireplace with wine and salted oregano crackers. The atmosphere was jolly, and once more we talked about our roads to Bremen. In those first days, we got the short versions, fragments of events, a swarm of details impossible to keep track of, but all just variations on the same theme: where we came from, where we had been when we discovered the repetition, how we had settled into the eighteenth, when we had met one another and how it had happened. All bits and pieces of a story that always ended in the same place: at our wrought-iron gate. As if everything had led to our meeting – four on one side, five on the other.

Now we began to retrace our movements in the eighteenth of November to see how they fitted together, and it was not difficult to explain what had happened at the station in Berlin. The reason no more missing-person notices were being put up at the ticket office was, of course, that Ralf had returned, and so we no longer sent requests to the station staff to have our notices posted, and by the time the three of them had finally decided to go to Bremen to investigate the matter further, we had long since vacated Ralf's flat.

When they arrived at the flat in Henselstraße, there was, of course, no one home. Still, they felt that their mission had been a success, because when – after wandering up and down the street – they suddenly caught sight of Ralf's name on the intercom, it was like finding Father Christmas's front door, with a nameplate and everything. But Father Christmas did not open up. They rang the bell, but no one answered.

Ralf laughed when they told us the story. Henry laughed too, and we all laughed again at the mystery of the two posters: that a misunderstanding had been the deciding factor that brought them to Bremen, because when Henry had been in Berlin, he had put up the two posters, selected a couple of underground stations where he had hung a few more, then spent the night at a hotel near Hauptbahnhof, and the next morning he had made sure that the posters were still there – one at either end of the station.

It was Marlice who filled in the last details of the story about Ralf's flat. They had rung the intercom a few more times and waited. Still nothing. They returned several times that same day, then again the next, but there was no one home. When they saw lights in the neighbours' windows in the evening, they asked both those in the flat next door and those in the one downstairs about Ralf Kern, but no one seemed to know much about him, and his windows were always dark.

After a few days, they had moved into an empty second-storey flat diagonally across from Ralf's place. From the living room there was a view of his flat, or at least enough of a view to be able to see the street in front of his building. The three newest residents had noticed that there was no light in the flat, neither in the morning nor in the evening, and at one point, when one of the building's other residents came out, they had managed to slip in through the front door. The flat's postbox was stuffed with advertisements, and among them was a single envelope, easily fished out and containing a key that fitted the door. The flat was clearly unoccupied, even though a few pieces of furniture still stood in the living room, along with some dirty dishes and a pizza box in the kitchen.

Now that they had come to Bremen and installed themselves so close to the elusive Ralf Kern, or at least to his flat, naturally they had to find him. Most of their time was spent watching the building – from the flat opposite, from the street and from a café just around the corner – and then one day, an unfamiliar car had pulled up out front. It was Sonia and Peter. Rosi had been standing at the window in the flat, and when the car suddenly stopped in front of Ralf Kern's entrance, she ran down the stairs and outside. Waving her arms frantically at the new arrivals, she dashed across the street and asked the man behind the wheel whether his name was Ralf.

Since his name was not Ralf but Peter, and after he introduced Sonia to her, she asked whether they had a problem with the eighteenth of November. They did. The same problem as us, Marlice added. And us too, apparently, said Olga, who had barely spoken until then.

She had got up – probably feeling the urge to go for one of her walks – and was now standing in the doorway while Sonia and Peter told us about their journey to Bremen. They said they had seen a poster – in Hamburg, though I don't think we ever had posters there, maybe they meant Hanover – it must have been one of those posters where the three of us had been edited into a photo of Ralf's building on Henselstraße. In any case, the house number was clearly visible in the picture, and after puzzling over the poster and the reference to the eighteenth of November, they had decided to investigate. Sonia had written down the few pieces of information that could be gleaned from the poster, she and Peter had gone to Bremen, located the street and the building without any difficulty – and driven directly into Rosalie Torpa's line of sight.

In the days that followed, not much happened. Peter and Sonia had moved into the flat, the five of them had got to know one another and agreed that Ralf Kern needed to be found. They took turns standing watch, keeping an eye on the entrance, two hours at a time, night and day, and then all of a sudden a car they had not seen before pulled up outside the building: Henry had arrived.

Rosi had just taken over the watch from Marlice, and from the window she saw a strange car filled with cardboard boxes come to a stop. She called Marlice over, and as she was phoning Peter and Sonia, who had gone out to shop but luckily were just around the corner, the driver – which is to say Henry – got out and let himself into Ralf Kern's building. Marlice rushed downstairs to the street, jacket over her arm and shoes in her hand. She quickly phoned Anton, and shortly thereafter, before she had managed to put on her shoes, she saw the driver of the strange car open the passenger door, place a laundry basket on the seat, walk around the car and get in behind the wheel. At about the same time, Sonia and Peter came running towards their car, which was parked down the street. Marlice, suddenly unable to decide whether she should call out to the man, hurried over to Peter and Sonia, followed by Rosi, who had also raced down the stairs. Just as Henry climbed in and began driving down Henselstraße, Marlice, then Rosi threw themselves into the back seat – Marlice with shoes in her hand, jacket over her arm, and still on the line with Anton, who was a few streets away, coming home to take over the watch from Rosi.

Henry hadn't been aware of any of this. Admittedly, not long after leaving Henselstraße, he had noticed a car stop on the tramline to pick up a passenger but apart from thinking it a stupid risk, since the next tram could come along at any moment, he had paid no heed to his pursuers. Besides, he was having to rely solely on his side mirrors, as the entire back of the car was stuffed with boxes of crackers and porridge oats, completely blocking his rear view.

Keeping a few cars between them, they had calmly driven through the city and out to the suburbs, where Henry had unexpectedly indicated, turned left and stopped in front of a large wrought-iron gate. He had got out, rung the intercom, and a moment later, when the gate swung open, he drove through, still oblivious to his pursuers, who had pulled over a bit further up the road as soon as they saw him slow down and indicate.

Now we knew that we were at least six people in the eighteenth of November, Peter said. And probably more, said Marlice. She had been certain all along that it was not Ralf Kern they had been chasing across the city. She could not get the picture on the poster in Berlin to fit with the person in the car.

When Henry, who quite rightly was not Ralf, had disappeared through the gate, they drove past the house, but there wasn't much to see, hidden as it was behind the wall and all the trees. They turned around, drove back and parked in front of the gate. After briefly considering whether they should leave again, they got out of the car and hesitated for a moment before Sonia rang the intercom – and the rest you know, said Marlice.

Ralf said we had been sure we were not alone. At least, he had been sure. Because if it had been only the four of us stuck in this November day, our meeting would have been far too strange a coincidence. So few among so many. Marlice said they had thought the same. That is, when she and Rosi first met, for a long time they had believed that it was just the two of them. That it was some sort of local anomaly affecting only them. Like a *microburst*, said Rosi, a sudden weather phenomenon, violent enough to throw planes off course or lift cars into the air and toss them aside. A kind of microburst in time, she thought. A leap or sudden turbulence or a localised time-tornado, if you will. Whatever you wanted to call it. If it could happen with the weather, then surely it could happen with time too, she argued. It wasn't until they met Anton during a trip to Poland that they began to believe there might be more people suspended in the eighteenth of November. Because if the same impossible suspension could occur in the middle of Amsterdam and in a small town in southern Poland, then surely it could occur in other places too.

And now we knew that this event had taken place at least nine times and in at least eight different locations. Nine people, each alone in the midst of the catastrophe. Alone with the shock. If a catastrophe without any dead or injured can even be called a catastrophe, said Marlice.

It is clear that she and Rosi have been together for a long time. More than once, they have used words they've had to explain to the rest of us. An *anastrophe*, that's what they had called the incident. Or Marlice had, and then Rosi had too. And Anton, after they met him. For it was no catastrophe, just an inversion, and that was what that meant: anastrophe. Their world had not ended, they had simply been sent back to the same day. Without tragedy, without any fallen or dead.

Marlice had studied Greek and archaeology, Rosi said, when Ralf asked for some clarification of the term, but Marlice hastened to say that she had left her studies a long time ago, long before her day ground to a halt. Ralf thought it a weird word – an unnecessary construct, as he put it. He has never felt any urge to call a hundred days a *centium* either, as Henry and I still do on occasion when we need to take long strides in time, but naturally, on our very first evening he had mentioned his BeDaZy project by name and explained it to the newcomers, and no one seemed to find the name or his idea – constructing a system to generate a better day – particularly weird. I remembered all of Ralf's concepts from our meeting in his flat. Were they also unnecessary, or constructs, or both? Perhaps he would argue that his concepts point forwards, not back, and that an innovative new structure is more useful than constructs of the past.

I also detected a faint sigh when Marlice's studies were mentioned, and Ralf glanced pointedly in my direction when I began asking questions, as if to make sure I would not steer the conversation off track. He does not believe that people with an interest in the dead are what we need most in our situation, and he was visibly encouraged when, on the first evening, Sonia mentioned that she was a doctor. She had been working in an emergency department when her time ground to a halt, and neither Olga nor I could help but smile when we saw how Ralf instinctively began nodding as she spoke – several nods in succession, shoulders slightly hunched so that they seemed to nod along – like a prompter in a theatre or a teacher during an exam when their pupil is closing in on a satisfactory answer to a difficult question but must be nudged towards the right words.

Sonia is the only one of us to have entered the eighteenth of November with a touch of drama. On the evening of the seventeenth, she had been working the late shift at the emergency department. It had been a busy night, and at one point she'd had to stitch a deep gash on a patient's chin, a rather nasty gash, she said. She had administered a local anaesthetic and normally would have waited a bit, but because it was a busy evening, she asked whether he would let her try stitching him straight away, even though the anaesthetic might not have fully taken effect. It might sting a little, she had warned. He had nodded, and she had begun suturing, as she put it. By the time she was halfway done, the anaesthetic had fully kicked in, and she was tying the last knot when the police suddenly burst in – two heavily armed officers who informed her that her patient was wanted for murder. He had been on the run for a long time, and a minor traffic accident had finally exposed him. He was not as badly injured as first assumed – the laceration to his chin, a sprained hand and a few bruised ribs – but an officer had recognised him when the police arrived at the scene and called for a patrol car, which had followed the ambulance, and now his days as a fugitive were over. Fortunately, Sonia was almost done, or else she would have been stuck suturing between a murderer and two heavily armed officers.

It was late in the evening. Sonia finished her shift at midnight, and a colleague drove her home. The next morning, she woke up to the eighteenth, an unremarkable day, though she was still a little shaken from the events of the night before. That evening, she had another late shift. It was a quiet night, but she felt off balance. When she woke the next day to an exact replica of the eighteenth, she was convinced that the events of the seventeenth had derailed her.

For Marlice, it had been different. She did not feel that something external had thrown her off balance, despite also working in the hospital business, as she put it. She had been working in a hospital laundry facility on the outskirts of Amsterdam, and on the eighteenth of November she had been fired for taking a hospital gown home. That is, she had taken a gown a few days earlier and grown so fond of sleeping in it that she had tried to take another. It was gown number two that got her caught. She believed it was the theft of the second gown that had sent her into the November loop. Her inability to be content with just one.

She had met Rosi in a park in Amsterdam. Rosi had been an au pair with a Dutch family and had just taken the family's two children to school when she noticed the fault. Her mornings were usually quite routine, and her second eighteenth of November had started like most other days. The parents had left for work, she had taken the children to school, and if there was anything unusual about this particular morning, it was that, for once, she had set off with the children in good time. That was probably why she had not realised that the day was a repeat of the day before. She only became aware of it when – just as always – she went to sit in the park after dropping off the children. From her bench, she saw a dog break loose from its owner and attack another dog. The same thing had happened the day before, and the owner of the aggressive dog had been distraught. This had never happened before, the woman told the owner of the attacked dog – which was probably true the day before, but after a second attack just as vicious as the first, it had to be a lie. It was this lie that made Rosi uneasy, because who lies so blatantly, and who would believe such an obvious lie? They were the same two dog owners and the same aggressive dog, and once Rosi noticed this repetition, it was not hard to see that everything was exactly the same as the day before.

Marlice and Rosi had met each other in the park a few hundred days later. Rosi had initially tried to carry on as usual, getting up to see the children off to school and picking them up again in the afternoon. She had told a friend about the day repeating itself, but the friend had not believed her. She had called her parents, who had urged her to return home immediately, but the next day they had forgotten all about it. Eventually, when her days had begun to feel dull and she discovered that she could withdraw her money again and again and do more or less whatever she wanted, she had moved into a hotel and called her employer each morning to say that there was a family emergency and she had been forced to leave during the night. The phone call became part of her morning ritual, often followed by a walk in the park, and one day she had met Marlice, sitting on a bench that should have been unoccupied. After they met, they had spent much of their time together, first in Amsterdam, and later leaving the city to travel, usually together, sometimes alone, but always returning to Marlice's flat near the park where they had first met.

They met Anton Janas in Poland, where he was visiting his parents, who lived in a small town in the south of the country. In his day-to-day life, Anton taught history at a secondary school in Kraków. But his father, recently diagnosed with Parkinson's disease, had just turned sixty and was celebrating his birthday. Most of the students at the school were working on a major assignment and would not have classes again until later in the week. Anton had arranged for a colleague to cover his remaining classes so he could stay a few extra days with his parents. They had celebrated his father's birthday and he had been due to travel back on the twentieth, but when he woke up early on the day which he thought was the nineteenth, it turned out to be the eighteenth again. He, too, believed that he had a part to play in the suspension of time – that he was gaining extra days with his father this way. He had been worried. Very worried, in fact. He thought that his concern for his father was what had sent him into the loop. Perhaps his desire to halt the progression of the disease had brought time to a standstill.

Anton had not gone anywhere, not at first, at least. He had spent his days with his parents, helping them around the house, doing repairs here and there, petting their old dog, painting window frames, although his father had been adamant that one should never paint window frames in November. Anton thought the wood was dry enough to paint, and once he started, his father had insisted on giving him a helping hand. That was when Anton noticed the difference: his father's movements had become slower, but the most remarkable thing was that the painting his father did had vanished overnight, and after a few days Anton insisted on doing the work himself. He felt his father needed to rest.

Later, Anton had gone back to work, taking over the classes his colleague had been covering for him and told the whole story to this colleague, who believed him, but only after Anton predicted a few events from the eighteenth. Together, they tried to get to the bottom of the problem with time but had not been able to solve the mystery. Anton also met his ex-girlfriend and told her about his father's illness and about his eighteenth of November. She too believed him, without him having to provide any proof. Plenty of sympathy, no help, he said. But what could they have done?

During the weeks that followed, he had alternated between staying in Kraków and at his parents' house. When he was with his parents, he would take the family dog for a walk every morning. That was how Marlice and Rosi had come across him. It was during one of those periods when they had been on the road, travelling in Poland, moving from city to city. Normally, they would check into one of the larger hotels, where the many guests and a changing roster of receptionists made it easier to claim that they had arrived the night before. At smaller places, it was more difficult. You know the problem, I'm sure, said Rosi. There you are in the morning, having to explain your presence. Or you sneak out, then come back in as if you'd only just arrived.

Rosi and Marlice had arrived in the town early in the morning and checked into the only hotel they could find: a family-run establishment near the town square. Because the owner was running the place alone, and the only other guests were an elderly couple, they would not have been able to explain their presence in the morning. They'd had to slip out before the owner woke up and return a little later, pretending they had just arrived. They had spent the waiting time in a bakery that had a small café with a few tables and chairs set up in a bay window overlooking the street. Here, Marlice and Rosi would sit before heading back to the hotel to check in again. Since things went smoothly, and since they enjoyed exploring the town and going for walks in the surrounding countryside, they stayed for several days, and every morning they would have coffee and apple pancakes there, looking out onto the neighbouring houses from the bay window. One of the houses belonged to the Janas family, and it was on one of these mornings, when it struck Rosi that there was far too much variation occurring across the street, that they realised they were not alone.

Each morning, Anton took the family's elderly dog for a walk, always at roughly the same time, but some days he would come back carrying the old creature, setting it down only when they reached the front step. Other times he would return with the dog on a lead, and on one occasion, just before reaching the house, he had removed the lead and let the dog walk to the front door at its own slow pace. They had not seen such variation before. That is, they had not registered it until now, but that morning Anton came walking down the street with the animal in his arms, and when Rosi detected this variation and drew Marlice's attention to it, Marlice ran outside and asked Anton to put his dog down. There was something she wanted to speak to him about. He looked at her, confused, not grasping what she meant. He had never noticed the two women having breakfast across the road every morning, but soon he understood what was going on, and after thinking it over for a few days, he left with them.

It had been a little difficult to organise his departure. He didn't want to worry his parents and had initially found it hard to leave them. Whenever he stayed in Kraków, he had called them early in the morning to tell them that he'd had to leave before they woke up, but would he remember to do so every morning if he left them for good? Rosi had managed to solve the same issue with the family she worked for, after she and Marlice had explored the mechanics of things. She had written a letter, kept it with her for so long that it no longer disappeared from where she left it, and one night she returned to the family's home and placed it on their kitchen table. Anton did the same. In fact, he wrote several differently worded letters, carried them around with him, one for a couple of days, another for three, and eventually, it worked: one of the letters, his original draft, remained in the house, even though he himself had gone with Marlice and Rosi to spend the night at the hotel. And now his parents read that letter every morning. Or at least he was positive they did, he said, because on the rare occasion that he called to make sure everything was all right, they had already come to terms with his early departure.

Again, we sat in the drawing room late into the night, sharing stories of our November days, our unexpected meetings and the mechanics of time. Ralf spoke of his chance encounter with Olga on the side of the road, while Henry described the series of coincidences that had led him to a lecture on supply chain reliability in the Roman Empire. I no longer remember exactly how Sonia and Peter met. I think I was growing tired by the time we got to the details. It was at a hotel. Or a nightclub. Or perhaps they met at the hotel and ended up at the nightclub. Either way, they had been at a nightclub and left together. There was nothing unusual about that. While they had been alone in the eighteenth, both had occasionally brought a fling back to their hotel room. It had been simple: casual affairs that would ideally begin early in the evening and end before the night was over – preferably, they would say goodbye to their flirtation or date, or whatever they called it, well in advance to avoid any unnecessary confusion. Everything would, of course, be forgotten the next morning, but they could do it all again if they so wished. Easy, no strings attached, Sonia said.

When they met, they both assumed that it would be just another such rendezvous, of which the other would remember nothing the next day. Neither had suspected anything was amiss when they first laid eyes on each other, but no sooner had they got to talking than the truth became clear: that they would not forget in the morning, that both of their memories were intact, that they were alone but no longer alone, that they were two of a kind – all the things the rest of us thought too when we first met another person in the eighteenth of November. And yet, not quite the same, for theirs was a lovers' meeting and they had been together ever since. They had no intention of going their separate ways. Not ever. Not even if they could return to a normal time. If they were to go back, they would go back together.

It was obvious that they would have liked to share more details, as they have revisited the miracle of their meeting several times since their arrival. All those days, filled with a love that grew ever stronger. That they had lost all interest in returning to progressive time. They had never imagined it could be so easy. That love could be so simple. That one could find such peace in the company of another person. That sort of thing. But it's as if our minds start to wander when they begin to tell us their story. Ralf starts asking about Peter's work as a freshwater biologist before the eighteenth of November, or we grow tired, or Henry suddenly remembers something he needs to collect from somewhere. Perhaps we simply need to have their story told a little bit at a time. It's hard not to think of longing and lost love. I'm sure Henry's thoughts turn to his son and Martha Atlings when they're speaking. I haven't heard Rosi or Marlice insist on hearing more details either. Maybe it is easier to hear about lonely days in the eighteenth, about unease and confusion, about attempts to navigate the repetitions of the day, than to have to listen to their great love story.

I think of Thomas, of our time together, but that was long ago. I remember how it was, but I have no need to hear a similar story when ours has disappeared into a long tunnel of

November days, and theirs is happening right here. Maybe we just need to get to know them a little better. Maybe one has to grow a little fonder of them before they get to sit there, bathed in so much happiness. But that probably won't be too difficult.

1921

It is felt in the morning as we wake. The house stirs. We drift towards the kitchen and settle around the large table in the conservatory. As though we are a group. A flock. A gathering. Or at least, that's how it feels.

It is in the way things move. Cutlery and bowls making their way to the table. A hand reaching into a drawer for a handful of spoons, the sound of metal. The drawer sliding shut again. A cupboard opening, a stack of plates balancing in a pair of hands, then other hands bringing cups to the table. A pot of coffee is brought in, then another. Tea, brewed by Sonia, carried to the table by Peter, poured by Rosi, and Henry gets up to fetch milk while I take the empty coffee pot back to the kitchen and return with a full one.

It is this intertwining that makes it feel as though we are a group. The voices in the room, the eyes sweeping the table and the objects migrating from the kitchen to the conservatory. Then someone asks whether Olga is up yet, or whether anyone has seen Peter. Someone answers, or throws out a guess across the table. More questions follow, another scan of the table. Would anyone like more tea, are there any more oranges, and is there anything else I should bring up from the basement? Sentences floating, a voice replying, sometimes several at once. Yes, on the table in the kitchen; or no, she's still sleeping; or he was here just a moment ago; and then the coffee's ready, are there enough cups? And new questions come up, followed by comments on the questions and an answer from the other end of the table. We speak into the air over the table and answer on behalf of one another. We check to see whether we're out of bread, and someone mentions that the lamp in the upstairs bathroom needs a bulb, and then someone else remembers seeing a box of old light bulbs in the basement.

It is an open space. There is no need to set rules or make plans, we simply weave ourselves into what is already under way. If spoons or a trivet for the large dish just out of the oven are needed, someone will find them or bring something that can be used instead, teaspoons or a chopping board from the kitchen.

It is rarely clear who is doing the clinking and balancing, opening and closing. Or sometimes it is, because if someone takes out a tray and sets it on the table in the kitchen, if they stack plates and bowls and cutlery before carrying them in, then it's probably Sonia, or maybe it's me, because I have also taken to stacking. And if you hear someone yelp when they burn themselves on a pot or a baking tray, it's usually Henry, as he often uses damp tea towels instead of oven mitts, but most of the sounds could be made by any one of us.

It is not so different from when we were only four. And yet, in some ways, it is. The days were simpler. We more or less had assigned seats in the conservatory, not exactly, but our habits and routines were more stable. Ralf typically went off to work in the morning, but if he was home and the car was not in front of the house, we assumed Henry had gone out for supplies. We knew that if it was morning, Olga was likely still fast asleep in her room, and if she was not home at night, she was out walking. I could often be found in an armchair by the largest window in the drawing room. With a blanket tucked around me and usually a book or stack of papers in hand, or simply taking in the view of the lawn sloping down towards the stream at the bottom of the garden.

Now pieces of information are always floating around the house. The breakfast table is a place where sentences can be set aside. The kitchen is a place for exchange, some bring provisions, others turn those provisions into meals, which are then brought to the table, and people arrive and sit down, eat and tidy up, our digestive systems break down the same dishes, our brains hum with the same sentences, our words take on the hue of other words. It is an ongoing entanglement, all day long our bodies seep through the house, exchanges on the stairs, conversations and catch-ups in hallways and doorways, and in the evening by the fire, we sit and unspool all our days, long chains of the past, the time in the eighteenth and the time before the eighteenth, our whole lives, pulled into the room with us, where sentences float about and we trade gestures and movements. And sometimes, we talk about the time after the eighteenth. Not often. A remark as we get up and retreat to our rooms, or a stray thought as we lie awake, each on our own yet still together in the eighteenth, together in thinking of the nineteenth, perhaps.

There is much we do not need to explain. Everyone knows that we are using up our world, that we must tread carefully if we are not to become monsters and ravaging locusts. We know that anything new is finicky. That it takes time to make things stay put. Everything that once seemed bizarre and confusing has become normal, because we carry the same experiences and they no longer give us pause. Our distant families and lost connections, friendships that have been left behind, love that has crumbled, all that we once faced alone has become shared, it has all become a given. It is simply how things are.

Peter and Sonia sleep in the last room at the end of the hallway on the first floor. Rosi and Marlice have each taken a room of their own but are already fantasising about fixing up the chauffeur's cottage and moving in there. They believe more people will come. There are so many posters with our information scattered around, and if there are others like us, it's only a matter of time before some of them make their way to Bremen. Peter and Sonia are convinced that they have already seen some of the others: five or six people who did not fit the pattern of the eighteenth. They reckon it won't be long before the house is full.

They had been in Milan, sitting at a café in an arcade near the cathedral square. They had noticed a group of people in the square, or rather, Sonia had – one of them in particular, a woman in a yellow jacket. She had thought that she would fancy a jacket like that herself, maybe she had even mentioned it to Peter, but they had been talking about something else, or were simply too engrossed in each other. In any case, they had not realised until it was too late: that this group of people did not belong in the regular pattern of the Duomo square. When they returned a few days later, both the group and the jacket were gone. It was Sonia who noticed it: that she hadn't seen the woman in the yellow jacket, and although it was the same time of day, there was no sign of the woman or her group. They could interpret it only one way – that there must be others trapped in the eighteenth, either this whole group or part of it. It could have been a single person who had diverted the others from their pattern, but they believed the most likely explanation was that they had seen a whole group trapped in the eighteenth.

It was after a longer stay in Italy that Sonia and Peter had caught sight of the poster with Ralf's name on it. They had travelled north, to Hamburg or Hanover, or wherever it was, and they had assumed that the poster would lead them to the group with the woman in yellow, but instead, it led them to Rosi and Marlice and Anton. And to us. And none of us has ever owned a yellow jacket.

1928

Ralf wishes there were more people in the house. His project requires participants and information – not yet, but soon, he says, once the technology is ready. He still goes to his office, though not as often. He has long since started asking our new residents whether they have come across any critical incidents. Naturally, they have. They've told him about fires and traffic accidents and a heart attack in the middle of the street. Most have tried to intervene and prevent the accidents of the eighteenth, but to no avail, because the next day it all happens again. On one of her very first days in the eighteenth of November, Marlice had seen a plume of smoke rising from a basement window close to the park where she later met Rosi. The flat's residents had forgotten a pot of frying oil on the hob, no one had been hurt, but the residents – a family of seven in two small basement rooms – had lost everything, she said. And when Marlice and Rosi went to the park, they usually remembered to knock on the basement window and draw attention to the dangerous pot shortly before the fire broke out.

Most regard Ralf's project with a sense of relief. That they can hand over the day's accidents to him. It is hard not to dwell on the accidents one knows about, said Sonia. That one allows them to happen. That one cannot help. Or that one does not know what actually occurred. She remembers a certain drowning accident – or perhaps it was not a drowning at all – at the harbour in Naples. She and Peter had travelled from Milan to Naples, and on their first evening out in the city, they had walked along the waterfront. Around midnight it had begun to rain, and they took shelter under an awning. Suddenly they heard someone shouting for help. It sounded as if it came from the water, from beneath a pier or somewhere behind a moored boat. They rushed over and could clearly hear cries for help and the sound of someone in the water – or, at least, that's what they thought they could hear. They contacted emergency services and reported what they had heard, but others had already called for assistance. Soon, a rescue team arrived in boats, and a little later a helicopter hovered above. A beam of light swept across the water, first in the harbour basin, then further out, but there was no sign of the victim, and after some time Sonia and Peter had gone back to their hotel. The water could not have been cold enough to be life-threatening, but still they were uneasy.

The next evening, they had gone back down to the harbour. They had walked along the water and stood in the rain with their umbrellas, near the spot where they believed they had heard the cries, but there was nothing to hear. They had wandered around the area, but nothing happened, and they were no longer sure where the sound had come from.

The first few days after the incident, they had returned to the harbour several times, but still nothing happened, and it seemed that no one had fallen into the water. Peter and Sonia were now convinced that they were not alone. That others, too, were breaking the pattern of the eighteenth of

November. It could have been someone from the group in Milan who had been in distress at sea, or who had made it to shore and disappeared before the rescue team arrived.

Ralf wasn't sure if what they had experienced could be considered a critical incident. Had there been an incident at all? There had been a cry, but is a cry an incident? And if the person in distress had been one of us, it would, at any rate, fall outside the scope of the project, he said.

Ralf has prepared a form we are to fill out when reporting a critical incident, preferably with plenty of details and precise data. He wants phone numbers for witnesses and contact details for friends and relatives. He wants information on passersby and is compiling numbers for rescue services and emergency operation centres to ensure help can arrive in time. One of the most important fields on his form, apart from time and place, of course, is the one he insists on calling interference potentials, and recently he has added several more columns to his form, allowing us to suggest both digital and analogue ways to prevent accidents. His form contains several terms I have never come across before, some of which are surely of his own devising. As though he believes his plans can be implemented more successfully if the professional terminology and technical vocabulary have been established.

This morning, when Ralf once again insisted on talking about his project – perhaps in a little too much detail and maybe with slightly unrealistic expectations of those who had yet to arrive and to whom he could delegate tasks – Olga gave me a sceptical look, but I don't see how Ralf is doing any harm. Or how there would be anything wrong with us becoming more.

Of course, it is possible that we will never be more than nine, but none of us believes that any more. We could also stop here, Olga suggested later as we went upstairs. Or, rather, she stated it, because I don't think it was really a suggestion. She said that we could retrieve our posters and pull up the drawbridge. She only said it to me, but added that she wasn't sure if she meant it. She'd had the thought. So had I, but why shouldn't we come together if we are trapped in the same day? Being alone is always an option, I said. Besides, she herself had once hoped that there were others in the eighteenth – or at least, that's how I remember it. She didn't remember that, but yes, she said, being alone is always an option. She could move back to Ralf's flat for a while if she wanted, I said, but I don't think she wants that. She has her nocturnal strolls. And her solitary mornings. There are many ways to withdraw. If she wanted, we could go to Düsseldorf together, I said. For a few days. We could take the train, or one of the cars if she wanted to drive. I miss the medlar tree and my sunshine.

1940

But Olga is neither unfriendly nor dismissive towards our new residents. On the contrary. She bakes bread and makes jam. She has shown them around the neighbourhood, which she knows well from her many walks, she ties her hair up with colourful elastic bands, she drinks October beer from the basement with Rosi and Anton, and afterwards she takes long strolls in the dark of the night. Sometimes Anton goes with her, sometimes she stands in the kitchen with Peter and Sonia, but it's clear that she enjoys her discussions with Rosi the most. She doesn't really get Marlice, she says, but I don't get why she doesn't.

Nor did she seem to have any doubt about Chani Lydai when she suddenly appeared at the gate. I had just woken up and could see her from my window on the first floor. The gate was open, but she didn't come in. After I found a jumper and put it on, I heard footsteps in the hallway. It turned out to be Olga – already up and fully dressed. I asked whether she wanted to go down to the gate to fetch our new resident, as there was someone out there who had obviously gone astray. She said she didn't want to but then went down straight away, and moments later they came laughing up the driveway.

Chani was a nighttime rambler, like Olga, and had observed her on one of her nightly wanderings. Olga could walk for hours, and at one point, their paths had crossed. That is to say, Chani had seen Olga from a distance and followed her, not because she thought Olga was stuck in the eighteenth of November like herself – she couldn't have imagined that – but because she was curious to know more about this fellow nighttime rambler.

Chani lived in a flat in the city and had been organising conferences for a living when her day came to a halt. Originally from Konstanz, she had studied biology, like Peter, but grew tired of her studies and moved to Bremen after being hired by a science museum. She had been tasked with organising an exhibition about biological structures in industrial design: car doors that resembled bird wings, chairs inspired by spider webs, plates shaped like plants. That sort of thing. Here, she had met her boyfriend, and when the exhibition ended she stayed in the city. She had got a temporary position at a conference centre while continuing her studies in Bremen but never finished and instead carried on organising conferences. Later, she had moved out of her boyfriend's place. The usual, she said: projects and short-term roles and relationships that fall apart. But then time had ground to a halt.

Now she went on long walks at night and slept during the day, unless, on rare occasions, she felt the urge to go to work at the conference centre. One night, during one of her walks, she had spotted Olga and followed her for a few minutes, thinking nothing of it other than that here was another nighttime rambler, maybe just someone on their way home. When Olga turned down a street Chani hadn't planned to take, she gave up the pursuit and let Olga disappear into the distance, still curious but convinced that this nighttime rambler would reappear, at the same time and in the same place. It wasn't the first time she had noticed someone on her walks, followed them and found out where they lived and who they were. Out of sheer curiosity, she said. An interest in the strange ways of other people. Or boredom.

A couple of nights later, she had returned to the same area, but this time Olga was nowhere to be seen. Nor did she show up the next time, and several nights later, when Chani finally spotted the nighttime rambler again, there were suddenly two of them, because Anton had come along, and furthermore, the timing was off. Chani had quickly figured out what was going on: that they must be caught in time like she was, or at least one of them was, because maybe the new rambler had been pulled out of their pattern. She herself had sometimes pulled people out of their patterns. She had visited her ex-boyfriend and had gone out to eat with her friends in the city. She had visited family, as many of us do. She had gone on holiday, as she called it when she travelled away from Bremen for a while. But she had never encountered anyone else who was astray.

Chani had trailed Olga and Anton at a distance, and when they reached the wrought-iron gate, it was open, because something was wrong with the closing mechanism. She waited until they had disappeared, and as soon as they were out of sight she walked up to the house. She watched Anton and Olga through the windows. She saw a light being switched off on the first floor, she heard a window being opened, and eventually the house went dark. She did not imagine that it was a house full of people, all of whom were stuck in the eighteenth. Why, she did not know. Perhaps it was just too hard to picture. It was easier to think that Olga and Anton existed in two separate times, that Olga had gone home with Anton and would leave the house before morning.

Chani had spent that night in the chauffeur's cottage, which Marlice and Rosi are in the process of renovating. She had stayed awake for most of the night, waiting to hear Olga leave the house, but it never happened. The next morning she returned to the gate, rang the intercom and waited for someone to answer. She came up with an excuse to ask for Olga, but it wasn't necessary, as Olga appeared and invited her in. As they made their way up to the house, Chani confessed that she had followed her on her nighttime strolls. Olga said that she already knew. She had seen Chani both times – and also noticed that she had followed her and Anton home – but she hadn't wanted to scare her off, she said, and then they both laughed.

I don't think it's true when Olga says that she isn't fond of the newcomers, or that she doesn't want any more to join us. Maybe she's worried that they will disappear again. I think of her unease when Ralf was missing, and I think of her mother. But then I think it might be me. Maybe it is all of us. Maybe we are all a little uneasy. About tremors and unforeseen changes. It has happened before: losing a world familiar to us. We know that we cannot be sure of anything. Or anyone. As if another person were a gift we must cherish.

1941

What do we think of one another? I do not know. Have we become friends? I think so. What else could we be called? Housemates? We are more than that. We are tied together by a shared history. Not a family history, nor a childhood story. We are not like pupils in the same grade: people bound together by birth year or geography. We haven't chosen one another or signed up for a club from which we can resign, we are not on a sports team that we can quit or be dropped from. It is not a workers' union, we are not classmates or colleagues. We are joined together by the unpredictability of time, or that is how we think of it – we have fallen out of the world, each of us plummeting, all of us dizzy. Our lonely wanderings in the eighteenth. And our meetings. Not being alone any more. All the things we do not need to explain.

1942

Our meetings, said Ralf. We were sitting in the car on our way to a paint shop to pick up paint for the walls, brushes and masking tape. We had been talking about how he and Olga had met on this very road leading into town. How he had come to a stop when he spotted a person who did not usually come wandering along the roadside. How she'd no intention of getting into a car that had pulled over to wait for her, hazard lights flashing. But he was also talking about the other meetings. We mustn't forget our meetings, he said. He talked about compulsory attendance and slips of paper in a cracked cup.

He had offered me the driver's seat. He was going to teach me how to drive. I said that I had never liked cars. I didn't like this steel-encased space, I said. The false safety, the hard shell. Moving at a speed that could crush the shell in an instant.

We have told the newcomers about our meetings. I do not know what they think about sitting there, holding meetings on topics we have collected in a cup, but Ralf thinks we should keep up the meetings. He wants to talk more about his project. He said he had put a slip of paper in the cup. Or two, actually. He thought it was important to talk about our opportunity to change the world. Or the day, I said. Our opportunity to change the day.

Ralf believes our meetings should have firmer frameworks. That we should focus on the most important things, that we should agree on talking points well in advance, that we should prepare, have agendas and topics and subtopics and not be guided by random paper slips. He said that we should find meeting days that were easier to remember, so that no one would forget to show up. He suggested that we move our next meeting to day # 2000. I suggested that we make the decision collectively. After all, things had been working fine so far. Except for that one time I forgot a meeting – but that was back when there were only two of us.

Ralf insisted. He said that he wasn't sure I fully grasped the scale of the task we had been given. That neither I nor the others really understood that there was a world out there in need of our care. Maybe the issue wasn't whether we understood or not, I said, but that it wasn't something we could fix with agendas and scheduled meeting days ending in zero. I said schedules and meeting preparations and pretzel sticks in a cup weren't the answer. But if the project was to gain momentum, he said, it had to be put into a more defined framework. We needed goals and subgoals and continuity.

Personally, I was more inclined to believe in random chance and a simmering enthusiasm, I claimed. That one must take action where one can, when one can. I began talking about excitement and seizing the moment and running with good ideas, that sort of thing. My own excitement, I said, had always been more of a gentle simmer, and my momentum like the sound of pebbles on the shore shifting with the waves on a calm day. The sound of pages turning. Quiet weather systems. A crackle in the fireplace.

I don't know why I said that. But now that I had started down that path, I kept going. To take part in a project like the one he was outlining, you had to believe in it. We had to find the right moment. We had to remain alert, let the ideas grow naturally.

No doubt the people in distress would be absolutely thrilled about that, he said. That one had decided to wait for the right moment. And listened to the pebbles on the shore. That one first had to paint one's walls and find the right colour, he said, because now we were approaching the paint shop, and I reached into my pocket for a list that Marlice had written.

He'd run the numbers, he said. How many people would be needed to get the first version of the BeDaZy project off the ground. The analogue version. The full digital setup wasn't finished yet, but we could begin with a smaller version. He'd soon have a proposal ready to pilot-test it. He had analysed several models, as the best approach was not immediately obvious. Should we expand our radius of action step by step? Should we prioritise specific geographic areas? Should we start by focusing on the incidents that were easiest to prevent? Or should we, on the contrary, tackle the most difficult ones first?

I said that I felt torn between his urge to prevent very concrete incidents and Olga's hope of changing something more fundamental: that it was about the structures and the future – about the time after the eighteenth. The dilemmas he had just outlined didn't make it easier. I felt like I was being pulled in several directions at once. Fortunately, we had arrived at the paint shop. Ralf indicated and turned into the car park.

Once we had loaded four large buckets of white paint into the car boot, along with a large bag of brushes and stirring sticks and a colour chart with the full palette of shades, I said I would like to give it a go after all. He had already forgotten that he had suggested I take the driver's seat, but he obliged, and very slowly, once I had adjusted the mirror and received a brief introduction to the pedals, he released the handbrake and let me start the engine. He told me about gear changes and brakes and the biting point and the importance of fluid movements, and I eased my foot onto the accelerator – far too gently at first, because nothing happened – but soon enough we were on the road and moving steadily towards home.

Much to my surprise, it was not difficult. I asked about the car's braking system, recalling my Norwegian driving experiences. I told him about Jeanette, my taxi driver, and the system that prevented the brakes from jamming. About how our car had started to bounce and rattle when the system kicked in. That it saved us from colliding with a large blue lorry in the opposite lane. That it felt as if not just the vehicle, but existence itself had begun to shudder. Not like when time came to a halt. That was different. But rather, I said, the way I imagined it would be if time abruptly started back up.

Ralf said that on a dry, snowless road, I didn't need to worry about that. He asked me to flick the indicator on and off, he said right and left and straight ahead, and all of a sudden we were at the gate – which, for once, was closed. I think it's Peter who has repaired it.

Ralf instructed me to pull over, got out, punched in the code and while the gate opened he got back into the car. He made sure the coast was clear before allowing me to cross the road and drive through our gate.

When we were sitting in the drawing room that evening, I insisted on talking about cars. Marlice would have preferred to talk about the colour chart we had picked up from the paint shop, and Ralf wanted to discuss the possibility of doing a test drive of the analogue version of his system. Peter asked whether he had doubts about the feasibility of the digital version, but mostly it was a matter of the time frame, Ralf said. He believed it was important for us to have a preliminary version ready, in case time suddenly resumed its progress, as he put it. We wouldn't want to be caught off guard, and then we began to discuss the chances of returning to progressive time. That's a subject we rarely broach and the conversation did not last long.

I think it was me who brought the conversation back to motor vehicles. I insisted that a car was not a means of transport at all, or at least that its actual function was something else. After all, weren't our vehicles first and foremost a form of protection? I could hear how it sounded – as if I were now entitled to all sorts of opinions about cars just because I had sat behind the wheel once, but I felt compelled to explain what I meant. Had the family car not prevailed precisely as the institution of family was beginning to crumble? Suddenly every family had to have a car: the patriarch at the wheel, the mother beside him, the children tumbling about in the back seat, and thus the fragile nuclear family travelled around inside its own protective box. As if the family unit could be held together simply by packing it into a metal tin and setting it in motion. The patriarch had become invisible, he had become a wage earner, absent from the family all day, but when he was off work, they all got into the car and no one could doubt who was the head of the household. But by then, it was already too late. The family was changing, and soon the whole thing collapsed.

I could tell that no one really understood where I was going with this, so now I turned my attention to all the cars that drove around with just one person inside them. The urge to sit in one's own vehicle. A person enclosed in a capsule. Wasn't that the same thing? Isn't that what we do nowadays: we do not stick together, we sit there, separated and uneasy, individuals without direction, selves at risk of crumbling, and so everyone must have a car. A self-car. A thin shell, but a shell nonetheless. A contraption for those with insecure identities who crave a more robust armour than that which is built from within. People think that the car is a means of transport, I argued, but it is not the engine that gives the car its value. If that were the case, people would never accept the hassle of owning one: the costs, the risk of being killed or injured or causing accidents, the endless traffic jams and parking problems and visits to the mechanic. We would not put ourselves through all that if it were simply a matter of transport. It is the body of the car we need, I said, not the engine. The engine is just an excuse. We claim that we need the car to get from A to B. In reality, we need it to hold ourselves together.

Now everyone had something to say about cars. Sonia had often thought that people who did not want to drive were the ones who did not want to take responsibility for their lives. For themselves, or for the family, perhaps, if I was right about the family car.

Rosi objected. Was that really what she thought? Roads packed with responsible drivers, and pavements and bike paths full of people who did not take responsibility for their own lives. Surely it was the other way around. Did she really believe that world history was full of irresponsible, directionless dimwits until the car was invented? Were drivers not just people trying to get ahead? At the expense of others? Was that what taking responsibility looked like? Or was it more about barrelling your way through the world, putting on armour, puffing yourself up? You laid responsibility aside when you got into your car, she said. You surrendered your soft mobility. The self in armour. Crusaders of capitalism. Was that what taking responsibility meant?

Henry couldn't quite see the contradiction, because after all, he said, hadn't I merely claimed that we tended to use our vehicles to uphold society's fragile structures, that we used them to protect something in the process of crumbling, and then we began discussing what it was I had actually said. In any event, he remarked, it was incumbent upon him to point out that my assertions lacked empirical evidence. Why the car, of all things? Why not start with the chariot? What about the prairie wagon, full of household utensils and tools and a cradle for the little one? Did it spell the end of the pioneers' era? And the ships – what about them? Gigantic container ships, did they mark the end of global trade? Was I suggesting that this urge to collect the world's goods in gigantic vessels signalled the era's imminent demise? The last breath of world trade? Did I mean more generally that by looking into the transport sector's protective boxes, one could determine what was in the process of dying?

You forgot aeroplanes, said Rosi. Just look at them. What are they for, if not to see the world from above? Quite literally: to elevate oneself. To feel superior. Are they a means of transport? Or are they rather tools for maintaining the idea that some people have the right to see the world from great heights. How many people fly because they actually enjoy it, or because it's necessary? Not many. Most do it just to cement their status: companies sending out representatives to promote their brand, researchers asserting their position at conferences, corporate leaders meeting to make decisions that could just as easily be made over the phone, holidaymakers travelling to avoid a loss of social prestige for themselves and their children by not staying at home.

Now Henry talked some more about empirical evidence and a little bit about sunny weather, but he was interrupted by

Marlice, who would rather talk about paint cans and colour charts than all our boxes and capsules and tins.

1945

We have held a meeting about pillows and bedcovers. About basements and chalk. It is Peter who is interested in limewash. Marlice wanted to discuss cushions. She believes the house demands to be furnished with style.

When the meeting began, Ralf had suggested that we update the structure of our meetings, and he had outlined a new set of rules, but there was little support for this. Most preferred to continue as we had when there were only four of us. Or with just a few adjustments. Perhaps we should stick to a single topic, said Anton. Henry thought two was manageable, but selected well in advance of the meeting so we had time to prepare. Rosi, on the other hand, believed our attention to the world sharpened when we didn't know what we were going to talk about, and if any facet of existence could become the subject of an entire meeting. Sonia wanted the meetings moved to a day that would be easier to remember. Numbers ending in zeros offered natural beginnings and endings, she thought. She must have spoken to Ralf about it, but Anton instead suggested that we introduce special holidays, for example on days ending in zero. Peter enthusiastically suggested an additional topic for the day's meeting: planning future parties and celebrations. Once he had said this, there was a moment of silence, because that's how it is: our future lies in the eighteenth of November, there is no prospect of anything else, and we might as well start planning festivities and events far into the future.

But if it was to be its own discrete topic, Peter would have to wait and suggest it for the next meeting, said Rosi, who sat with the cracked cup, ready to draw the topics for the day's meeting. The first topic turned out to be Peter's own suggestion: renovation of the basement, a project he had already started and for which he needed assistance. The next topic was stylish home décor, which Marlice had proposed.

When we finished discussing whether Rosi had been coached beforehand and whether the slips of paper in the cup were marked in some way, which both Marlice and Peter denied, we embarked on the first topic. The discussion didn't take long, because all Peter wanted was a plan so he would know whom he could count on for help, and one or two volunteers to investigate how to solve the problem of painting the basement walls, which had previously been limewashed but subsequently painted over without fully removing the lime. Ralf and I promised to investigate. We knew the way to the paint shop where we could probably get some advice, and Ralf thought I needed another driving lesson if I was going to become a capable driver.

The discussion of the topic Marlice had put in the cup was more lengthy. First, we needed to clarify what Marlice meant by stylish. I feared she was about to start browsing design shops and reading interior design magazines, that she wanted brand-new cushions and luscious fabrics and elegant sofas where neither crumbs nor wine would be welcome.

But that wasn't the case. She had found curtains in the basement, which she wanted to fashion into bedspreads and cushions and covers for the shabby sofas. She had found fabric scraps and brocade and old ball gowns in second-hand shops, and together with Anton, she planned to set up a sewing room in one area of the basement and a furniture workshop in another, once Peter had completed the renovation. She had noticed that all of us had worn-out clothes we hadn't wanted to throw away because they had been with us for so long, and because it was easier to keep them than to buy new ones. Our tattered clothes could be given new life, she thought. Some could be altered, the scraps could be used for rugs and cushions. She had several ideas, which she presented. She had proceeded methodically: she had acquired a sewing machine and tested new materials and fabric from second-hand shops and scraps from her own wardrobe, and she had observed that old materials – especially those we had carried with us for a long time – could help make the other fabrics stay put. Furthermore, things sewn by hand were more reliable than those sewn on a machine, and she was sure that careful needlework and reusing what we had lying around could make our world more stable. There are plenty of things one can do when sitting in a drawing room in the evenings, she said. We could sit there and stitch our pasts together; everything we had been through alone could be pieced together anew.

Henry wasn't sure he wanted to sit around and sew bedspreads out of people's worn-out clothes, and in any case, he didn't think it was such a problem to spend a few days getting things to stay, and Ralf agreed, arguing that it would take up too much of our time. His project required people to be available, as it would take many working hours to complete within a reasonable time frame, but Marlice didn't see the issue. Quite the contrary, handiwork encouraged reflection and conversation on important matters, she said.

It is apparent that Ralf thinks we should be putting more effort into preparations for the time after the eighteenth, but most of us don't believe that it's urgent. It is hard to prepare for something you don't believe will happen.

Once we had finished discussing the two topics, Ralf pointed out that we still had time for a couple of his project's most pressing issues, but then Rosi suggested that the remaining slips of paper in the cup should be pinned up on a special noticeboard in the kitchen. That way, we would be reminded of all the other topics between meetings, because, of course, there was nothing stopping us from discussing those. And what's more, she added, it will be obvious if anyone puts several slips into the cup to increase the likelihood of a certain topic being drawn. As she said this, she unfolded not just one, but two slips proposing Ralf's project as a topic – both in the same handwriting.

Or makes small marks on them, said Ralf, who was fiddling with that day's two slips, running his finger over them. You could both see and feel a small pinprick on the back of each. One read *Pillows and bedcovers*, the other *Keller und Kreide*, and on both slips the dot from the 'i' had pierced the paper. Funny, Ralf remarked, that by writing in German, Peter had given himself a dot. Had it read *Basements and chalk*, there wouldn't have been one, though really, in German, it should probably have read *Keller und Kalk*, he added. One doesn't paint walls with chalk. I said that he could have written *Limewash and paint*, and then Rosi would have had two dots to guide her. Anton supported Rosi's suggestion of a noticeboard in the kitchen, where we could hang up all the suggestions from the meetings. That way, no one would feel overlooked.

I do not know whether the suggestion of the noticeboard was approved, but I think it was, because Ralf was nodding along with Rosi. Marlice wrote the project on our to-do list, Henry didn't protest, Chani and Olga, who hadn't said much, exchanged a glance that I couldn't quite decipher, but they seemed amused. And Tara? She went out to the kitchen while the others continued their discussion, put the kettle on for tea and got cups from the cupboard.

While I waited for the water to boil, I tried to remember what the various participants in the meeting had said. There is an expectation that I will keep a record of how we spend our days. Or at least some of what goes on in the house. The most important parts, at any rate. They think I write more than I do, but there are always blank periods when I write nothing – or perhaps just the odd note or two. Still, I notice a great deal. And there is a lot I remember.

1971

It is not just because we live here together. It is not just the house or the shared fridge. It is not just the noticeboard where our slips of paper are pinned up. It is not just the mornings in the conservatory and the grey light that gathers the space around us. It is not just our exchanges and all our sentences and the way we relate to one another.

It is also the way we connect with the things. It is the paint in our hair after a day's work in the basement, it is sore fingers and calloused skin from upholstery needles and fabrics. The furniture has been stripped, and Rosi and Anton have begun the reupholstering. Sofas and armchairs stand there naked, some upside down, with springs and webbing scattered across the floor. It is the stuffing that has been removed. It is the protective slipcovers that have been peeled off, and the old furniture fabrics that have been carefully cut away. It is hessian and canvas and flock wool that makes people cough, it is piping cord and passementerie and dusty rosettes. It is long rows of nails that are prised out with pliers and clipped off with cutters. It is armrests and chair legs that are dismantled, cleaned and sanded. It is small tables that Chani has found and sands, paints and varnishes.

Henry has joined the furniture workshop. He has started sanding and staining. Fixing trims and legs and gluing wobbly armrests. I think he had started to feel left out. The endless ferrying of provisions, all his foraging, which had become a solitary pursuit. Not because no one wanted to keep him company, but usually he just set off on his own. He said that it was all that remained of his connection to the world outside the house. Standing alone in a market or a warehouse. Trying to explain that he wanted to save wilted vegetables from being discarded or prevent bags and boxes and tins from being thrown out. All that was left over: unsellable goods, surplus stock, miscalculations. He feels that we live in a sheltered world, and it's only there – in front of the vegetable stand at the market, in the warehouses with unsold goods, in the small front offices of importers, in the cold storage rooms full of too much milk and yogurt – that you feel some slight connection to another world, he says. That's where he accepts his losses. Maybe that's why he goes alone. To negotiate with a world that is lost.

Olga has started helping Peter with the basement renovations when she isn't busy with kitchen work. The sewing room, which we have set up in one of the largest parts of the basement, was painted first, and the upholstery workshop was inaugurated a few days later. Now the next nooks are being fixed up while Marlice and Sonia have got to work in the sewing room. Marlice designs, Sonia sews, and often I help by cutting the fabrics or ironing, folding and tacking. They don't sew just bedspreads and cushions – once they start, they can't stop. They sew clothes for anyone who needs them: dresses and shirts and skirts and bags made from fabrics they have found. They cut up tattered tablecloths and sew dishcloths, they make oven mitts and tea cosies and whatever else we need in the house.

In the evenings, Chani often moves one of her tables up into the drawing room, and then we sit there with busy hands, cutting and sewing and varnishing, as we talk about things we have seen and incidents we might prevent, and most of the time Ralf sits ready with his pencil, noting down all the things that go wrong.

2028

There is room for more people here, and more people are joining us, and we have enough furniture to accommodate them all. It is the basement rooms of the house that have drifted upwards. It is the newly upholstered furniture, and it is the heavy curtains that have been fashioned into cushions and bedspreads. It is the shelves in our larders now lying bare. It is boxes and bags that have disappeared. The tins of tomatoes – chopped and with basil or chilli – have been eaten.

The wine cellar has been nearly emptied, and even the old tins of carrots and peas have vanished. It is cardboard boxes stained with rust rings that are empty and, even though the dates were illegible, so far none of us have got sick. It is the last jars of bockwurst which are gone. The platter had to be passed around the table several times, but all of it disappeared in the end.

Sometimes, when Olga or Peter or Chani has been busy in the kitchen, things begin to move in the opposite direction: when they have baked and pickled and dried and preserved the surplus fruits or vegetables, then jars and tins drift the other way, but not for long. Soon they float back up, and the boxes procured from the world outside the house seldom make it any further than the pantry behind the kitchen.

There is a balance to uphold. Olga keeps count, Henry gathers supplies, and often I go foraging with him. We must travel further afield, because we have emptied the nearest stores and need to source greater quantities. We have found small-scale importers, we have picked up Catalan delicacies and Italian pasta products. We visit wholesalers and producers that have poorly managed logistics, and we find a use for most of what they have. We bring back crates of soups and sauces destined for the incinerator, sacks of rice or flour, all of which we need now that there are more of us. We lug boxes and set them down in the hall, and I chop wood and stack it into piles in the shed.

On the floor in the living room in front of the fireplace lie cushions sewn by Marlice and Sonia. Now most of the beds have bedspreads, and rarely do more than a few days go by after a new resident arrives before another bedspread begins to take shape. We use scraps from the reupholstering and we cut clothes into new shapes. We stitch ourselves into the materials of the house, interlacing our stories. It is not just our movements that get tangled, our imitations and emulations, the way we curl up on the sofas. It is not just the cloud of questions and answers hanging over the breakfast table or our constant interaction with things, our shared work on the objects of the basement. It is also the things themselves merging, ingredients fetched and carried and chopped and sliced and turned into meals; it is the connection between things; it is the furniture dotted about the house, the newly lacquered tables put in the oddest places, corners otherwise dark illuminated by old lamps, rusty or carefully polished, with old fabric shades soaked until the water turned brown from the cigarette smoke of residents long gone, traces of their breath still lingering in the curtains and lampshades. All these exchanges and connections.

It is a house that is open. The world wafts in through the cracks, like rain or snow, materials settle in the rooms as though there existed other weather than the grey sky after all. Almost like seasons: there is leaf fall and snowfall, old layers falling away, pieces of furniture shed their fur, benches slough off their skin, and suddenly there's a sofa in the kitchen, an armchair in a bathroom, a seat under a window, with cushions and new colours, brightly springlike.

And people trickle in, new residents, alone or in small groups, snow in flurries, a winter congregation from the north, a summer flock from the south. I think of them as weather, as wind or snow. They ring the intercom if the gate is closed or walk up the driveway and knock at the front door, they bump into people on their way in or out, and the newcomers hang their jackets in the hall and take off their shoes or wipe them on the doormat.

Now we are no longer just the ten we became after Chani arrived. Now there is Lenk Hamon and Karna Jeri. There is Aisa Klein and Martine Paran and Narita Harding, who arrived together. There is Tona Granec and Marc Pillon, who arrived by bicycle, and who have gone about finding more bikes and fixing them up so we can always get around without a car. There is Milly Arcmole and Adriano Richter and Sarah Trent. There is Norman Enser and Thea Sander, who, though they knew each other, arrived in separate cars. I hope our next meeting will be about vehicles, because now we have six cars and only two of them work. Fixing them is difficult, because repairs often come undone overnight. Ralf has had some success by sleeping in his car after it was repaired, so it still works, and Thea bought her car shortly before she met Norman. It hadn't been easy to make it stay. She and Norman spent several weeks in it – they slept in it, drove around in it and parked in a garage and lived in it. She believes it's the weight of things that makes them hard to hold on to, but I think of the heavy pieces of furniture in the house, and they're easier to make stay than a coffee grinder, I said. And we need the furniture, while the cars just sit there, taking up space. If more people are coming, I hope they come without cars, or that our next arrival is a mechanic, but according to Ralf, it won't make a difference – cars have become too complicated, the spare parts are the issue. You can't simply make do with replacing a single component every now and then.

But Ralf does want to find a mechanic, he says. And others, too. He still needs assistance. He has put up a notice on his door on Henselstraße so anyone who comes looking for him in Bremen will know where to find us. The notice has a tendency to vanish, but each time, Ralf hangs it back up, and most of our new residents have come via Henselstraße. All of a sudden, here they are. I don't know if Ralf has been out hanging more posters, but he has admitted it was he who put up the ones in Hamburg. As though he were searching for himself. Henry had brought the leftover posters with him to Bremen when we convened at Ralf's flat, and while Henry and I were in Düsseldorf, Ralf drove out to put them up. He wanted more helpers, and they arrive little by little, alone or in groups. The gate is mostly left open now. Once in a while Olga closes it, but she isn't the one removing Ralf's notices from the building on Henselstraße. It must be the wind. Or maybe it's me.

2046

We have held a meeting about sprouts and things that will grow. Anton and Aisa had proposed the topic, because they had made a frightening discovery, they said. Or not exactly frightening, but strange. Or surprising, at least.

It was some potatoes that had caught them by surprise. Henry had bought several crates from a market, most of which we had eaten, but one crate containing a few blighted potatoes had been forgotten at the back of a kitchen cupboard, and while tidying up Anton and Aisa had stumbled across them: somewhat shrivelled and sprouting little pale shoots.

In principle, it should not be possible for things to start growing, Anton said, or in any case none of us had witnessed it before. Even the biologists among us thought it made no sense. Peter was certain he would have noticed such behaviour in plants had it occurred. Chani believed it must be the unique properties of potatoes which enabled them to overcome the day's suspension. Their ability to sprout of their own accord, without water or light, almost regardless of the season.

They had made the discovery ten or eleven days before our meeting, and Aisa, who sleeps in one of the rooms behind the kitchen, had taken responsibility for the potatoes, laid them on a plate and kept them moist. After a few days, during which they had unmistakably continued to grow, she had dug up soil from the garden, filled some large pots she had found in the shed by the garage and planted the potatoes. When we gathered in the conservatory yesterday, there – in a line down the centre of the large table, beside the cracked cup that held our suggested meeting topics – stood seven large plant pots. Although we did discuss the topics from our cup, and the remaining ones were pinned to the noticeboard in the kitchen, most of our meeting was spent discussing the seven plant pots now lined up before us with little dark-green and quite crinkled potato tops.

What exactly had made them grow, we could not agree on. We spoke about the chocolates that had turned grey in Ralf's kitchen cupboard, and the small larvae that had perhaps, perhaps not hatched in an old bag of rice when Henry and I were living in Düsseldorf together. We spoke about the irregularities of the day and whether it might be possible after all to grow a garden in the eighteenth of November. Chani believed we should look into the biological processes. Did growth occur only in certain plants, such as the potato, or was its scope broader? She would like to investigate that.

Marlice felt that we were overstating the strangeness of the matter. After all, if you can keep clothes from vanishing by wearing them for a few days, and if you can hold on to brocade fabrics by carefully sewing them together by hand and stitching them to materials already carried into our day, why shouldn't you be able to make a potato sprout? Posters stay up or disappear and library books remain where they are or return themselves depending on how they're handled. If the world could be trained or coaxed or cajoled, she said, why couldn't you kick-start biology too? Why couldn't a house full of people make a potato plant grow? She was sure it was the bustle of people, our nighttime conversations, the pickling and preserving séances after dark and the crowded kitchen during impromptu midnight snack parties. Our mere presence. That we had become so many. Perhaps we have simply made time pass. Together.

Sonia was quick to suggest that we conduct further research. A production of microgreens would be a good place to start: sprouts and shoots from peas and beans and seeds and grains – surely these could provide us with all the freshness and crispness we'd been missing? If we were successful, that is.

Aisa began to fantasise about turning the entire lawn that sloped towards the stream into a vegetable patch, but Chani insisted that, were it possible, the grass would have long since shown signs of growing – at least a tiny bit. It would have grown the way grass grows on grey November days: so slowly it's barely perceptible, yet still enough that the lawn would have needed to be mowed. That hadn't happened, not even as our numbers grew. Just as well, really, because the lawnmower buried in the corner of our woodshed is unlikely to start for anyone.

Of course, it wasn't just the grass that had stopped growing when the day ground to a halt, because no matter how hard we tried, we couldn't think of a single animal or plant that followed our time. Hair and nails grew along with us, just as they would if time were moving forward. Several of us insisted we could see new wrinkles when we looked in the mirror. But never had potatoes in our vicinity sprouted, and I was sure that neither the apple tree in Clairon nor the medlar tree on Wiesenweg had changed. I had occasionally eaten a fruit that had fallen from the tree, but without my intervention the trees stood each day precisely as they had the day before. I had seen leeks vanish from their row in the garden, but I had not seen anything grow. I was fairly certain of that.

Maybe there are too many of us, Olga said. Or just enough, Chani said. Enough to spur the world into growth. And then our conversation turned to everything we hoped to grow, and a little later, after the shortest meeting ever about the two topics from the cup – one being the use of old incandescent bulbs we had found in the basement and our possible overconsumption of electricity, the other being the issue of worn-out credit cards – we made a list of potential sprouting scenarios to try out. We didn't get around to discussing cars or our health, though Sonia had proposed the topic several times, but the kitchen noticeboard is swarming with white slips and we have ample opportunity to discuss them all outside meetings.

When the meeting was over, Chani and Aisa went out with Henry to procure plants and seeds, and as soon as they returned, the first batch of sprouting seeds was placed in water to soak. On the way back from the store where they had found the seeds, they had stopped at a nursery, as it had occurred to Aisa that we could grow our own fruit. At this time of year, she reckoned, in November, it would be possible to get hold of citrus trees with fruit merely needing a little companionship.

They came back with five trees, which they carried into the conservatory, each one bearing fruit just waiting to ripen in our company. A couple of the trees had buds, and Aisa was convinced they would soon bloom. Some of us had – perhaps a little optimistically – imagined waking to the scent of citrus this morning. But of course, nothing had happened. Nothing had unfurled, and I'm not sure citrus trees can blossom their way through November days.

2092

Aisa believes we need to be patient. We know that our seeds can sprout and that our sprouts can grow, and for now we are not asking for more – not for lawns and not for orange blossoms or lemon blossoms, because the grass is at a standstill, it is unlikely we will get it to grow, and in the conservatory the trees show no sign of change. You make do, Henry said, when Sonia yet again buried her nose in the crown of the lemon tree. The little buds are still there, they haven't withered or fallen off, but nothing is happening.

Yes, you make do, Sonia echoed, with a glance at Peter. She plucked a leaf from the tree, snapped it in half and sniffed the torn edge. Peter said nothing. I hope they're not having problems. We need all the love we can get in the house. If we are to keep our faith in love, that is. Even though I feel longing or sorrow when I hear about the happiness they have found in the eighteenth of November, I cannot imagine anything worse than it all falling apart. Then I wouldn't know what to believe any more.

2172

Jeanne Fraizon and Pia Karlevic arrived last night – with no car but in high spirits. They had passed by several times without stepping through the gate even though it had been open, but as it happened, yesterday, on the day they finally decided to venture inside, the gate was locked.

They rang the intercom: three short buzzes followed by one long one. First once, then almost immediately again, until people came rushing outside to find two women at the gate – one holding a nearly empty bottle of champagne, the other waving an unopened one in the air.

They were let in straight away but were mildly alarmed to discover that there were so many of us. After all, they had only brought a single bottle. The issue was swiftly resolved when Olga retrieved provisions from a special corner at the very back of the basement where several wooden crates of champagne are kept, and later that evening we had to go back for a few more.

Jeanne and Pia accompanied Olga to the basement, where they were given a tour of the sewing room and upholstery workshop – now rarely used, since the house no longer lacks furniture, and recently turned into a bike repair shop instead. They were shown the laundry room and the drying room and the storeroom with its nearly bare shelves and the soon-to-be-empty wine cellar. Very little remains in those parts of the basement still holding objects from the past, and at this point there are only a few corners with old filing cabinets we have yet to clear out.

Over the course of the evening, Pia and Jeanne were introduced to most of the house's residents and were surprised by how many of us there were. They had noticed people around the house, observed lights switching on and off and us coming and going at random, but they hadn't expected there to be quite so many of us – and we knew even more, Olga said, after they had brought up fresh supplies from the basement and begun working out how many residents we could accommodate in total. Maybe this is just the beginning, Ralf added. Let's see what the future holds.

Pia and Jeanne suggested we convert the basement rooms into bedrooms. They'd be happy to help, if they could stay. Naturally, they were welcome. Someone is almost always off travelling; just recently Peter and Sonia left and Norman Enser has moved into their room.

Olga has discovered that several of the neighbouring houses are empty. Lights switch on in the windows at night, but we never see anyone inside. At first she thought it was just the usual pattern of the eighteenth of November illuminating the windows: people turning lights on and off throughout the evening, but there is no one home, just a timer controlling darkness and light. She noticed that lights always came on exactly on the hour. No human does that, she said, no one looks at the clock and says it's eight on the dot, I'd better turn on the light.

She believes there are several houses we could take over as our numbers grow. They're easy to spot, she said, and there are plenty of them. All you need to do is watch for the lights. That's the good thing about rich people, Pia said. They never actually use their houses. And when they're not in use, they're ours, said Olga. Including the wine cellars. They just sit there uselessly, waiting for the nineteenth. Or twentieth.

2237

Daniel Ramma arrived alone, a few days after Jeanne and Pia, and so early in the morning that I was the only one awake to greet him. I had got up to put Olga's rolls in the oven. She rarely bakes these days, but she had been persuaded when someone made a special request for her morning rolls, their crunch and perfect crust, so that morning three trays were waiting in the fridge: almost forty rolls ready for the oven.

I had put in the first two trays, and they were almost done when I heard a faint warble from the entryphone. Two short rings, so I went to the door and saw that the gate was closed. I buzzed it open and walked down the driveway, and there he was, Daniel, clearly freezing. I don't know where he had spent the night, probably on the train, since he had arrived in Bremen that morning.

I greeted him at the gate and we hurried back to the house. He didn't understand why we were in a rush, but he followed me inside, and only when I pulled the two trays of rolls from the oven did the urgency become clear. The rolls on the top tray were a bit too dark, almost burnt, the bottom ones slightly too pale, but Daniel was hungry and wolfed down two of the darkest ones before he had even had a chance to tell me where he had come from or how he had found us.

I quickly picked out a couple of the best-looking rolls and placed them on a plate, which I carried up to Olga's room. Daniel asked if I was the mother of the house. Not really, I said, but I had always felt the need to look out for Olga. She often forgot to eat breakfast.

Daniel struck me as younger than most of us. I soon learned, though, that he is older than both Olga and Rosi, as he had been over twenty when his day came to a halt, but he seemed young. Hesitant at first, maybe a little shy, but not for long, and I think he decided on the spot to move in. Now it feels as though he has always been here.

That morning he had just arrived from Spain. He was still cold even though the kitchen was warmer than the rest of the house, so I crept up to Henry's room and asked to borrow a jumper. Henry was awake but not yet up. I told him we had a new resident – shivering and just in from Andalusia.

Daniel pulled on the jumper and ate two more rolls, one pale and another of the darkest ones. I did the same and then it wasn't so obvious that I had left the top tray in the oven a little too long. Daniel helped prepare the rest of the breakfast, carefully mixing a range of shades into each bread basket. By the time the others came downstairs, we were baking the final tray of rolls, which, thanks to Daniel, came out just right: neither too pale nor too dark. He offered to help with the baking, and when Olga turned up, she gladly handed the job over to him – and to Chani, who volunteered at once. Now, every evening, or most evenings at least, you'll find the two of them in the kitchen kneading dough, and in the mornings they're up early, baking rolls for everyone.

Not until this evening did I find out who Daniel was. Or rather, where he had been living. I had curled up on one of the cushions by the fireplace; it was warm and I had grown tired, eventually dozing off while the others carried on a conversation I had only heard the start of. Now and again, I would stir, catch a snippet of what was being said, only to drift off again, until suddenly I heard Daniel describing one of the houses he had lived in.

At one point, he had stayed in an abandoned house somewhere in Spain, in Andalusia, I think it was – that much I already knew – but now he began to describe the house in greater detail: how he had returned to it several times, and how he had realised someone else had been living there. He had left his keys on the kitchen table and kept a basement window ajar so it could be opened from the outside with a light tug. He hadn't wanted to carry his keys around while travelling, in case he lost them. Why he had bothered locking the front door, he couldn't say – obviously, no one ever came by.

Olga laughed and said that he wasn't the only one. Maybe most people locked their doors – Tara certainly did. I think it must have been the mention of my name that made me realise I had been half listening as I dozed, and straight away I knew exactly where Daniel had been living.

I heard him explain that the basement window had been latched from the inside when he returned to his house. After a few centia, he said, as he's one of the people who speak of centia, perhaps because he feels some tie to Henry, whose jumper he has worn since the morning he arrived. But the door had been locked and the basement window wouldn't budge, he said. He hadn't wanted to smash the glass and was worried that someone had been living there. Or might still be.

That night he had slept in the garden shed and the next morning, when the sun rose, he had found the keys behind a small pile of bricks. Right next to where he had been sleeping.

Someone had lived in his house while he was away, which couldn't have been possible unless there were others who had ended up on the wrong side of the eighteenth of November. At first the thought had unsettled him. He had locked his doors and made sure to keep his windows shut at night, but increasingly he had felt the urge to find this other resident. He had started calling her Goldilocks after he found a toiletries bag with a few hair elastics in the bathroom and assumed she must be a woman. Or a girl, he said. She had lived in his house and slept in his bed.

And sat in your garden furniture, I said. And listened to the sounds of night. Joggers and grandmothers. And a staircase with steps that creak.

He admitted that he had become obsessed with the thought of finding Goldilocks. And then, as it turned out, it was just me, I said, once we had finished laughing at the unlikely coincidences. Or maybe he had turned into Goldilocks himself, I suggested, recalling the episode with the burned rolls, which I tried to work into the story of *Goldilocks and the Three Bears*. But although he had eaten both the rolls which were burned and those which were too pale, neither of us had touched the last tray of rolls – the ones which were just right – because by that point we were both too full.

It's strange to feel this sense of kinship simply because you have lived in the same house, I noted, and then we spoke about the garden furniture, the sounds of night and the small market where we both bought fruits and vegetables. We spoke about the moon's shadows. I don't know why I remember it so clearly. I had wondered why the moonlight had been so bright.

But how did we end up in the same house? He didn't know. It looked like a house that had been abandoned, he said. Abandoned, but not dilapidated. That's often what our homes are like: habitable, but uninhabited. And then we discussed all the prerequisites for moving into somewhere new. The houses couldn't be too big, nor too small. Not too close to the neighbours, but not too far from a town where you could find food. There had to be shops of a certain size so as not to be constantly reminded of how we're emptying our world. The area couldn't be too deserted but not too overrun either, as there needed to be enough life nearby to avoid feeling lonely, without feeling crowded. Maybe it was not so odd that we had ended up in the same house after all.

2246

We were supposed to hold a meeting yesterday, but I'm not sure you could really say that we did. Our last meeting had been skipped because we were busy refurbishing the rooms in the basement, but now we had agreed to assemble and put our slips in the cracked cup. It turned into a meeting about everything, because no one kept to the topics at hand. People wanted to discuss all sorts of things: one another and the time before the eighteenth, practical matters, the cleaning of toilets, rubbish and shopping, the cars that would never start and which I can't see the need for. Perhaps only one, I said. They just sit there, taking up space. We discussed the words we use, the vocabulary of the eighteenth, and the number of days.

The day began in chaos. Quite a few people had forgotten we were meant to have a meeting, and not until the afternoon did we finally gather. Our conversation was going off in all directions, and despite efforts to establish some structure, set a speaking order and keep things brief, it didn't work. Even Olga insisted that we stick to the day's topics, but it proved impossible. Everyone offered adjustments and additional remarks on the two topics we had initially drawn, and eventually we emptied the contents of the cracked cup onto the table – sestertius included – and talked about everything.

Many feel we are missing words – that is, we have enough words, the house is overflowing with them, but they are imprecise. There are too many things for which we lack terminology, and it is difficult to come to an agreement. Apparently, before we can find the right words, we must discuss everything at great length, with everyone speaking all at once.

In the end, we decided to hold another meeting today. Not just because everything had become too chaotic, but also because Gita Kreis and her group showed up. Or at least part of it – nine new people joined our meeting, though I think they know about sixteen people altogether. They arrived from Liège, where they live on a deserted university campus, and they had heard about us from Tona and Marc who had visited them there.

Actually, Marc and Tona had been on their way to Paris. By bike. But during a stopover in Cologne, they spotted one of our posters and reconsidered. Initially they had continued towards Paris but couldn't shake the thought of there being others in the eighteenth of November, and when they reached Rochefort, they agreed to change course and head for Bremen instead to look for Ralf Kern. Or perhaps for those searching for Ralf Kern, since who knew whether Ralf was still alive?

En route they decided to spend the night in Liège, but when they reached the outskirts of the city, a sudden downpour forced them to take shelter at a bus stop. Once the rain let up, they had looked around and discovered a deserted campus, rather dilapidated, undergoing either renovation, demolition or both. Everything was cordoned off except for one gate with a broken lock. They snuck in and headed for one of the buildings and suddenly there was a whole group, or three or four people at least, who knew who they were – or perhaps not exactly, but they knew they were stuck in the eighteenth of November. It was a safe assumption, as no one else came through that gate.

When Gita's group appeared there, on the gravel, among the puddles, and said they were stuck in the same eighteenth of November, Marc and Tona assumed there must be some connection between them and the posters. But the residents of Val Benoît, as the area is called, had never heard of Ralf Kern and knew nothing about the matter.

It was Gita Kreis who had found the place. Or rather, she knew it from the time before the eighteenth of November, as she had occasionally trespassed to take photographs of the abandoned buildings. After time came to a halt, she had returned every so often and eventually moved in. At first she lived there alone, but one night Jahn Herat and Charles Jomlin had shown up. The two had already met Mayte Matson, who arrived a few days later. At some point Gita had met Jane Voss and Karel Varbek on a train. Helena Ibart had turned up later on and, not long after, they were joined by Hera Leng and Nirmala Holst. Recently a whole group who knew one another arrived, but they had left again.

Tona and Marc stayed for a few days, and when they left for Bremen, they promised to contact Gita if they found Ralf Kern. Or others. And they did: they found Ralf, and they found others and they contacted Gita Kreis.

Gita's group is considering moving here. Or at least attending the meetings. If there are sixteen of them, as they believe – or eighteen, counting Tona and Marc – then altogether we must be around forty people in the eighteenth of November. If we include some of those people whom the new arrivals have met along the way, and if the five or six people Sonia and Peter saw in Milan are also stuck in the eighteenth, then there are nearly fifty of us in total. But there is no longer anyone who believes that this is our final number, or that there will be enough room in the conservatory if everyone turns up.

This morning there were twenty-nine of us around the table. We had got hold of more chairs, and the rest of us perched on the sills of the bay windows overlooking the garden, in the grey light from the sky. There was no end to the possible topics of discussion, no end to the suggestions for our decision-making procedures and agendas, no end to the digressions and additions and ideas that branched out in all directions. And though it would be a stretch to say we arrived at any conclusions, we did manage to keep to a handful of our topics. More or less, because when we were finished no one really felt that we had reached either consensus or clarity. But we had tossed a jumble of thoughts into a common pool.

It turned into a meeting about the names of things, about the words for the peculiarities of the eighteenth of November, about the chances of ever finding terms that truly fit, about precision and the spaciousness of language, and today the sestertius came in handy. When our discussion was at its loudest, with everyone talking over one another, Rosi suggested using it to decide who had the floor, though, really, a die might have been more practical, as there were usually more than two people who wanted to speak at the same time.

It all started with a debate as to whether a centium was a good word for a hundred days. Someone asked how long we'd been living in the house. About four centia, said Henry, quick to respond, or roughly a year, if we'd still had years, and with that, the discussion was in full swing because how does one mark the days in a time without years or seasons, and how does one divide a run of days when neither weeks nor months have any meaning?

I told the others about the time Henry and I began to use the term *centia*: how it gave us a new tool for understanding the days. Scissors for cutting time into large chunks. Suddenly we could take big leaps in time, bundle our days into units of time and give ourselves over to the fantasy of a distant future. As if we were here to stay. As if this were a time we could share. Where would we be in two centia if the days kept repeating? Or in three? What did we want from our future? When would we meet again?

Sonia thought it was fine to talk in terms of days and centia, but we were missing a smaller unit for our day-to-day planning. She suggested that we might use *decia*, or possibly *decims* – that ten days was a reasonable unit of time. When it came to divvying up household chores, for example. Ten days seemed an appropriate span of time to be in charge of cleaning our bathrooms, cooking our meals or washing the floors. A ten-day period was manageable. Or five, suggested Martine Paran. Ten days was two handfuls, but what about a smaller unit. The most tedious tasks could be allotted for blocks of five days. A handful of days. And we could call these units *decims* and *pentans*. We could start by allocating chores for decims, she said, and the jobs no one wanted could be assigned for pentans, and then we turned to discussing which tasks belonged in which category, but that, Jane Voss thought, was a whole other conversation. The residents of Val Benoît take a different view on time. Most of their minor household chores have been set aside while they focus on a large-scale renovation of the buildings. What mattered most, according to Jane, was that our units of time should be adaptable to a variety of situations in life.

Aisa Klein thought we should give the days names. She herself had held on to her weeks. She had counted seven-day chunks and stuck to the names of the weekdays, but this had become more and more difficult, and after meeting Martine and Narita, she stopped altogether. Aisa believed that if we were going to implement short units of time such as pentans and decims, we should also give the individual days new names. Otherwise, we would never be able to keep track of when one pentan or decim had ended and another had begun. Naming of this kind would be a considerable undertaking, she thought. Not just coming up with the names, but also agreeing on them. She would be keen to take part.

Some felt we needed a wider interval of time to describe our life in the eighteenth. Something equivalent to a year or even longer. We needed a way to capture the sense that we were growing older with the days. One doesn't get old in a centium, or not really, but most people felt they were ageing little by little as the days passed. Many of them had tried to count the years, but it was difficult without seasons or other changes to go by. When the days are all the same and there's nothing to mark the end of one year and the beginning of another. Some thought that the next unit should be called a *millium*, that we had entered our third millium and that it was palpable. Our age. A sense of being moulded by time. That time had etched itself not only in our memories, but also in our bodies. Changes that did not simply vanish. That sort of thing.

Most of us had thought of time as a long succession of days. A string of beads, Aisa said. Far too long if not broken up. And days that are all far too alike. Or a washing line thick with clothes-pegs, said Marlice. Peg after peg in long rows, and here and there a garment pinned to the line: days when something significant happened, moments that stuck in your memory. Or a tunnel, said Henry, a tunnel of days. A long stagger from pub to pub, said Mayte, who had met Charles and Jahn because they frequented the same bars in Venice. It had taken her a while to realise that something was wrong. That she and the boys, as she called them, were all caught in the same day.

I said that I had felt as though I were at the bottom of a well, with a rope that got longer and longer with each passing day. I had imagined that it would eventually grow so long and so heavy that I would be able to throw it back up. That someone would catch it and pull me out of my well. I spoke of the days as a kind of railing: that I had been intent on counting every bar, because missing even a day would make the railing unstable. The feeling that I would tumble into the chasm of time if the days were not all accounted for. I could also have spoken of a pile of days that grew bigger and bigger on the floor between Thomas and me, or of the days in time's container, of sinking down into the eighteenth again and again. But metaphors are not what we need, said Lenk Hamon, who was growing impatient. What we needed were words to encapsulate our days. We needed units of measurement, distinct time frames, precise terminology. For most of us it felt forced to refer to centia or decims. Not to mention pentans or millia, which just sounded weird. And what forms of the words should we choose, which languages should we use to feel at home in these words? We felt our way, tasting words, modelling suffixes, pronunciations and plurals, but we couldn't agree on what sounded most natural, because there was nothing natural about our terms.

Maybe we should seize the opportunity to ditch all that ancient flotsam and coin totally new terms, suggested Lenk. He argued that the names proposed were much too conventional, but this gave rise to so many outlandish suggestions that Rosi recommended we change the subject. I'm not sure we did, though, because we then fell to discussing why it was easier to name new phenomena than to give old phenomena new names. People were forever thinking up names for newborn babies, for companies and products, for ships and roads and houses and blocks of flats.

Or for new projects, said Peter, referring to the BeDaZy project, because no one has any issue with Ralf's made-up name once he has explained what it stands for. Admittedly, Olga did laugh when he first presented it to us, and we still can't quite figure out how to pronounce it, but now we use the name BeDaZy as if it couldn't be called anything else. Peter was duly corrected, however, when he called the project's name an acronym. Surely it was a syllabic abbreviation, Lenk said. Things have names, he insisted. An acronym is an acronym, an abbreviation is an abbreviation, and that became another point of discussion, until suddenly we found ourselves trying to come up with examples of genuine acronyms, as Lenk called them, and then someone proposed we name the world we came from – the life we had lived before the eighteenth.

TOL, for example, *The Other Life*. Gita suggested DAL, *Das Andere Leben*, but Henry didn't like that.

One of the Val Benoît residents suggested that we call time before the eighteenth *La Vie Avant* and the time after *La Vie Maintenant*, that way we could talk about *LaViA* and *LaViM*. This led us back to the difference between acronyms and syllabic abbreviations, until Gita's group pointed out that we also needed to address time after the eighteenth, *La Vie Après*, but that, too, would be *LaViA*, introducing unnecessary confusion – unless, of course, we could expect these two to be the same: that the world we return to after our life in the eighteenth would be exactly as before. Then they could share a name.

Like the morning star and the evening star, said Marlice, and then she had to explain: they were actually the same star – or rather, the planet Venus, glimpsed at different hours of the day, and Marlice and I immediately found ourselves wondering how the Babylonian astronomers came to discover that the two stars were one and the same. Had they found this out by observing the stars and the horizon, or by poring over their calculations and measurements? If, that is, it was the astronomers who made this discovery, said Marlice. Maybe it was already common knowledge: for sailors and shepherds and wanderers, and anyone else who spent their nights under the stars. Maybe they were well aware that it was the same star. Maybe the astronomers were simply the last to discover it. And suddenly we were moving along two different tracks: those who wanted to talk about the possibility of one day returning to the life we had left and those who wanted to discuss the Babylonians' knowledge of the stars. The latter discussion continued in the kitchen because Marlice and I went to fetch oregano crackers, the very last boxes from the warehouse that Henry has now visited so many times that there are no longer any crackers or porridge oats left. Gita joined us, followed by Daniel, and we ended up talking about the stars in the sky, that is to say, our own portion of it, which had to be there somewhere, hiding behind Bremen's heavy clouds, although we never got to see them.

While we were in the kitchen, the conversation around the table shifted from the chances of returning to the life we knew from the time before the eighteenth of November to the exact number of days we had been stuck. Could we even be sure that we had counted correctly? The majority had tried to keep a tally, but for many, there had been periods when they had lost track of time. Some had counted days from the outset, others hadn't begun until later and had resorted to guesswork.

Thea Sander had recorded all her dates in a book. Not the numbers of the days, but the calendar dates, as though the days had simply continued – which several people found unsettling. We can't use those days, Karna Jeri objected. They're reserved for later. They're dates that can be used only once.

We've got to save them, she said, for when we return to a world that contains the nineteenth of November.

Thea thought we could use them for celebrating our birthdays, but Peter felt that our own special celebrations should suffice. He and Sonja are back in Bremen. Sometimes they stay here, but occasionally they need a bit of time to themselves, so they have taken up residence in the flat across from Ralf's building on Henselstraße. Peter thinks we should have more high days and holidays but ones we invent ourselves, and Karna agreed: it would be far too depressing to base our celebrations on dates of the past. You can't spend an entire day dwelling on missing your best friend's birthday. Or your child's, said Henry, but he then fell silent, and before anyone could ask further, someone changed the subject.

And then came the inevitable question: what should we call ourselves and what should the others be called – those who woke up every morning believing that they were entering the eighteenth for the first time, that everything was as usual? The question tends to crop up when we're discussing the differences between us and them. There are those who refer to us as *loopers* and the others as *noopers*, and some speak of *repeaters* or *returners*, but that raises the question: who are the repeaters, really? Isn't the difference simply that we know we are repeating the eighteenth while the others believe everything is normal? But we see them going about their business, again and again. So who is the repetition? That was usually

Henry's line, but today I adopted it because Henry stayed quiet. Amongst themselves, Charles and Jahn had discussed *tracers* and *erasers*, having quickly discovered that they left behind a trail of empty bottles in the bars of Venice while the bottles drunk by other patrons generally stood untouched and unimbibed the next day. It had been a recurring topic of conversation between them: should they frequent a new bar where they could enjoy their favourite drinks, or should they forgo their favourite drinks and stick with their regular haunts? In the end – though only after banding together with Mayte – they had solved the problem by moving on. They had stayed in Naples for a while, and Sonia wanted to know if any of them had ever fallen into the harbour, since the mystery of the person in the water had yet to be solved. But none of them had. They only knew that they left behind traces of themselves. And that other people's traces were erased.

When several of those present launched into a discussion about whether a tracer could actually be defined as someone who left tracks – did it not refer to someone who followed them? – Henry, who had not spoken for some time, remarked that in Norwegian one might distinguish between *sporsettere* and *sporslettere*. The room fell silent as Henry slowly delivered these Norwegian words. For a second, it felt as though that was what we were: *sporsettere*. People began to roll the words around on their tongues, a hum of variously accented Norwegian filled the conservatory. Once the room was no longer humming, I told the others about the time I learned that the Swedish word for the Milky Way was *Vintergatan*, the winter street, and for a few moments we all sat there humming in Swedish, guided by Thea Sander, whose mother was from Sweden.

Now more people began tossing their own linguistic pearls into our common pool. We talked about words for particular moods, about the Russian *toska* and the Czech *lítost*. Daniel mentioned the Portuguese *saudade*, and Helena Ibart, one of the latest additions to arrive in Liège, told us about *dadirri*, a word she had learned of when visiting a friend in Darwin in Australia. It described a way of listening, she said: a peaceful attentiveness to one's surroundings, to the forest or the water.

She had often listened in this way when travelling. Also to people's voices. When the conversation becomes a form of music, she said. When you don't interrupt or try to answer or contradict one another. When you don't use language to agree or disagree or reach solutions and conclusions, but simply listen to what is being said.

After we had listened to one another for a little while, or rather, some listened and others offered more examples of words which did not readily translate between languages, Peter was eager to move on. He wanted to know whether we could find a word corresponding to our repeating day. Whether we should perhaps consider inventing a fitting term ourselves. Most of us call it a loop, a lap or simply a repetition.

Some speak of the day as a cycle or a circle, or else we talk about the retake and the remake of the day. Perhaps we could find just the perfect word?

Lenk Hamon didn't think so. He believes there are too many of us to be able to reach consensus on new words, since there would always be someone who didn't think a particular word was quite right. Some felt we should give it a try, while others thought we should first decide what we actually wanted. Were we aiming for words that could perfectly encapsulate a specific phenomenon, or words that were roomy and made us feel at home? And so the discussion flowed back and forth for most of the day. Some listened, others spouted cascades of suggestions. Some were eager to find a handful of words we could agree on and begin trying out straight away. To Olga, it seemed we had two options: give up before we even got going, or start from scratch and create a new language that could accommodate our extraordinary situation, but she agreed with Lenk: there were probably already too many of us to come to any agreement. We had too many different experiences, too many ways of seeing things. Even the languages that already exist lack precision, she said. We search for a word, but the words at our disposal aren't quite right. Language can make people feel excluded or forced into a certain mould. What may be a catastrophe for one person is perhaps merely a setback for another, Olga said, prompting yet another of our recurring debates: should what had happened to us be called a catastrophe, or would Marlice's *anastrophe* be a more fitting term? Should we invent something entirely new, or simply let it lie?

Many of us had known that it would come up, this discussion. Peter tried to sidestep it by insisting that without a shared vocabulary, we wouldn't be able to talk to one another at all. Could we not simply choose a word and adjust it later if anyone felt left out? But Olga couldn't see the point of adopting new words if they didn't feel precise to everyone from the get-go, and that, she argued, would only be possible if the words were spacious enough. Created collectively, with room for everyone.

Could we not have a few words to choose from, I asked, so each of us could use the word we felt was most accurate, and then just hope to be understood to some degree? That the roominess could be more in our minds, and not necessarily in the words themselves. I didn't think it was such a tragedy if I asked someone to fetch me a cup and they came back with a mug. What did it matter, I said, if our buzzer was called an intercom or an entryphone? As long as we could open the gate when someone needed to get in. But then Sonia said that if you communicated like that in an operating theatre, the patient could die. A cup is not a mug. And maybe what you really need is a beaker. Being precise, she said, looking at Olga, does not mean that words are roomy. Precision means that words are sharp. Sharp and narrow, ready to be plucked from a tray of surgical instruments.

But we had to be sure. This from Gita, attempting to back up Olga. There had to be space within the words themselves, not just room for everyone, but also knowledge and insight. We had to give them careful thought. How else could we know whether a word was right? You cannot simply adopt a word and demand that people accept it. How can we know whether our deadlocked day is a catastrophe or simply a turning point. If we are to find a word for what has happened to us, we have to understand what it is. She believed we had made too little effort to understand what had actually happened. Was it us? Was it something that had changed inside our heads? Was it the world itself that had fallen apart? All this we needed to know if we were to have any hope of finding words that were precise. We had all done a great deal of thinking, but had we examined the situation properly?

And besides, she said, she was not exactly sure what it was we were calling an anastrophe. Was the anastrophe the fact that the day kept repeating, that is, the day's daily recurring return, or was the anastrophe the original event: the actual break with progressive time, the seismic jolt that had shaken us all? Were we trying to describe an event or a state? In other words, had we been struck by an anastrophe or were we living in one – an anastrophic time? These were the sorts of questions we had to resolve first: we had to investigate the matter thoroughly and determine precisely what it was we wanted to find words for. Only then could we identify the right ones. Maybe we ought to hold a meeting about the phenomenon itself, our suspended day, and postpone the discussion of terminology until we knew exactly what it was we wanted to name.

Peter was insistent. There were limits to how much knowledge we could expect to have. Past peoples could see the sun rise, so they called it a *sunrise* because that was what they saw: an object moving upwards. Should they have investigated the matter, taken a more exhaustive approach? Should they have refrained from mentioning the sun until after Copernicus? Or later still? Should they have said that unfortunately they couldn't talk about the path of the yellow disc for another few thousand years, until someone had discovered that it was we, and the planet on which we live, who move around the sun? That it is not a disc, but a sphere. That it is neither yellow, orange nor red, but that the atmosphere lends it its colour. When do we know enough to give things names? When is it time to scrap the words we have and invent new ones?

He also thought that if it did not feel natural to use a word as simple and useful as *centium*, how could more cryptic terms ever catch on? Not that there was anything wrong with referring to centia or imagining hundreds of days spent together, but *centium*, he felt, was a festive word. We can raise our glasses and toast to our centia together. We can hold meetings and say another centium, come and gone, hip hip hooray. Which, by the way, he was all for. But if a new word was to catch on, it had to describe something for which we lacked words in our day-to-day lives. Could that be said of a hundred-day period?

I think most of us were aware that our discussion could go on for quite some time without getting us anywhere. That while we were all throwing our ideas into the mix, no one had any great desire to reach a conclusion. I thought of those foggy days with Thomas when we explored the world without really seeking answers. In a knowledge polka, a ballet of discovery, a tango of inquiry.

Perhaps we should talk about the passage of time, Daniel suggested. About aging. About how old we were now. If there was one word we needed it had to be the word for our age. Because when time does not pass and we cannot add one year after another to our ages, we have no words for the changes we undergo. Should we perhaps consider the term *bio-age*? Henry did not think this pertinent to the discussion and both Mayte and Chani thought the word was already taken and meant something else. Daniel pointed out that even if we could no longer talk about years passing, we could still celebrate birthdays. If we kept track of the years – which is to say, how many rounds of 365 or 366 days had gone by – we could simply add that number to the age we were on the very first eighteenth of November and we would know how old we were.

And that set us all off again: little chats on the windowsills and over the table, in the kitchen when someone took the opportunity to pop a few previously prepared gratins into the oven, in the queue outside the bathrooms when everyone made a dash for the toilet during the break. Everyone added about six years to the age they had been when the eighteenth of November came to a standstill, and everyone found themselves wondering whether people's ages seemed right. We sat round the table, seeing one another in a slightly different light. Did Gita look forty, and was Olga really only twenty-three bio-years old? We figured out that I was thirty-five and Henry was forty-three. Most people were surprised to learn that Ralf was thirty-four, because he looked younger, and come to think of it, shouldn't we have a party in three days' time, when Adriano would turn twenty-six? Should we institute rituals and traditions? A cake? Breakfast in bed and birthday songs? But by the time we had eaten and cleared the table we had forgotten one another's ages. There were too many of us to remember them all and our ages have no bearing on what we do, and so we resumed our efforts to devise a word for what had happened to us, and even though we weren't entirely sure about it, we couldn't quite let go of Marlice's *anastrophe*. It was probably wiser to use this word for the pattern of time itself, its way of recurring, but what we needed was a word for the fallout: what had happened to us. Most of us felt it would be an overstatement to call it a catastrophe and no one was satisfied with the more common expressions: a rift in time, the fracture, a temporal rupture, the repetition, the time warp, a calendar glitch, a chronological leap, the meltdown, the datal crunch, and whatever else we could think of. But, said someone – possibly Daniel – *anastrophe* was a pompous word, or no, it can't have been Daniel, it must have been one of the new arrivals, because Henry replied that this person was a bit too much of a newcomer to be calling anyone pompous, to which someone else rejoined that perhaps Henry ought to think twice before using the word *newcomer* in a negative way since it essentially divided us into two groups: the old and the new. As if certain people were more entitled to speak because they had got here first. Then we'd have to sit there around the table, assessing the worth of what people said based on when they happened to have passed through the wrought-iron gate and assigning value to a given suggestion according to how long its proposer had been here. And what other parameters would we then have to take into account? On what scale should a suggestion be weighed? The length of the sentence? The depth of the voice? Or its volume?

A new word ought to be a help, according to Jane Voss, who felt the discussion had gone off track. No matter who happens to suggest it. There has to be a hope of saying something more precisely with the new words than with the old; otherwise what's the point? This led to a discussion about what was better: a new construct that is precise or an old term that has been stretched and pulled and rendered spacious by years of use. And could old words be revived or combined with new ones? Here, Marlice's word, *anastrophe*, perhaps encompassed all of that: old and new, stolen and shared, with an essence that spoke of turning round, turning back. Granted, the word did have an old meaning, but of use that old meaning was not, she said. It was ready to be recycled. She thought we should see whether *anastrophe* would work. In spite of it being a construct.

Karna Jeri thought Jane was right. A construct it was, this anastrophe. That much was true. But was it precise? It was an obsolete word that we had twisted out of shape. We need words that we can feel, she said. She believes it must be possible to find a word that reflects what has befallen us. A chronological accident, a loss, a sorrow. She searched for words but couldn't find the right one. No, not an *accident*. A *misfortune*. Surely we could see the difference. She felt her way forward: *malheur de temps* or *time-misery*? Neither *Zeit-Unglück* or *Zeit-Unfall* worked, she thought – both made it sound too much like an accident. There had to be words that could contain the unhappiness of our situation. We could help one another, we could collect words from all the different languages we knew and see if the right one was to be found somewhere. A single word or a precise combination of words. The main thing was that this sorrow be woven into the fabric of the word itself.

That was how it felt when she was struck by the suspension of time. Sorrowful and unhappy. She had slowed to a crawl, her every movement had grown mournful. It sounded as though she had never quite recovered from the shock. She had never felt a sense of rebuilding, of inner reconstruction, of snow clearing, of sudden clarity. Of being rewrought for the task. She had never accepted the state of things. She had become despondent, not angry, not frightened, not uneasy or dizzy, just sad and bewildered that such a thing could happen. That it was even possible. She had never panicked, never concocted strange explanations or plotted bizarre escapes. She had never scrutinised the details of the day or felt relief about the extra time she was suddenly granted. There was only the sorrow of it having happened. A mute melancholy. A misfortune no one understood. She had told her closest friends, but even though they believed her, they didn't understand how she felt, and the less they understood, the more grief-stricken she became. For a long time, she had visited her two best friends almost every day, telling them the whole story again and again, the short version, the long version, but it didn't help. That is to say, it helped a little when they insisted on making her laugh. When they tried to convince her that it wasn't only a sorrow, it was also comical. That they could laugh about it together.

But it didn't last long. Even after her friends had cheered her up, after she had drunk coffee with them in their flat overlooking a sports ground from one window and an imposing church steeple from the other, after they had laughed and the mood had lifted, she would have to return to the streets outside, and already on her way down the stairs she could feel the weight of it. It was as if the entire city had turned to stone and steel around her, as if the materials had compacted. The red-brick church loomed like a mighty wall, and the sports ground resembled an enormous prison yard, tall grey poles and chain-link fencing that appeared to hold not air between its links but something else, some impenetrable substance.

She said we had to call the misfortune a misfortune. We had to tell it like it was. And we had to find the right words to describe ourselves too. Time-prisoners, in her opinion, was better than loopers or repeaters or returners – and to speak of tracers and erasers was to beat around the bush. Words like *sporsettere* and *sporslettere* were far too light and playful. The rhythm was off. We had to recognise what we were up against, she said. Imprisonment, walls, metal. Unhappiness and sorrow. The chasm we had fallen into. And our fate was doubly unfortunate, for even though time wasn't passing, we were still growing older – that much was clear. It is hard enough to accept the certainty of death. But to die on a day that repeats is to die in a deep ravine between two impassable mountain ranges. Who could be surprised by this sorrow, this void? Who doesn't feel the weight of this sadness? To find words to contain the unhappiness of our situation was the only way.

I said that there were probably many of us who had felt a sliver of this feeling. That I at least could recognise some of what she described. That I had wandered through the streets of Paris when I resigned myself to the impossibility of returning to normal time. When I understood that it was chronic. The city had felt strangely empty to me. It wasn't quite the same feeling as hers, but a feeling that it was physical, as if it were the streets or the buildings that had changed. Perhaps I didn't fully understand her, but her sense that it constituted a real change in the world's material – that, I understood. Or I understood part of it. I spoke about the feeling of having fallen out of the world. Having been discarded. Stowed away in an attic. I don't know whether she understood what I meant. It didn't look like it. I think she thought I was beating around the bush. That it wasn't her sorrow we were speaking about.

Rosi tentatively proposed that we speak of *anastrophe-sorrow* or *anastrophe-relief*. That way, she could talk about her sorrow without the feeling having to be embedded within the word. And at the same time, it would allow others the space to have different emotions. Maybe, if she could use the building blocks already available in the language, she could piece something together that felt precise.

Peter brought up the possibility of availing oneself of sentences. That she might say, for instance, that the anastrophe made her unhappy. Then everything wouldn't have to be contained in a single word or expression. After all, would she be any happier if others went around talking about chronological accidents and time-prisoners in merry tones? Or should we all learn to say the words with the exact same sorrow in our voices as she did? Would she be any better off if we found the right word for her? Wouldn't she run the risk of someone tingeing it with the wrong colour?

Karna didn't reply to that, and I'm not sure it would have helped if we had found the right word, or if one of us could have said that we had experienced the same thing she had. I don't think so. I think she will feel understood only when the language we use encompasses her feelings and her situation. Still, I can't help but think that being with others who are stuck in time like she is must be slightly preferable to being all alone. Because even if we use the wrong words, and even if we do not fully understand how she feels, we recognise what she is speaking of when sorrow enters her voice. We understand what cannot be put into words. I imagine that must help a little. But maybe I'm wrong.

Or maybe it helps to chop wood. One morning, she had noticed a pile of firewood outside the woodshed. We'd had a large delivery, so much that I hadn't managed to chop it all before nightfall and had given up, knowing the wood would probably be gone the next day. But in the morning it hadn't gone anywhere, and so there was no reason to rush. The pile remained, and when I passed by a few days later, Karna was busy splitting the logs. She had dragged the chopping block onto the grass, down towards the little stream that meanders by at the far end of the lawn. She had found an axe in the shed, and then she set about chopping one log after another.

Lately, I often see her in the mornings: there, on the lawn, with a view of the stream. She stands chopping wood, and in the evenings someone usually lights a fire in the fireplace, which we gather around, Karna too. It's usually Marc who gets the fire going, and before long he inevitably starts telling stories from his cycling trips with Tona. I don't know how many of his stories are true, but no one really minds. Tona tends to slip in a little later, and she rarely contradicts him even though everyone can tell that all of it can't possibly be true. No one can reconstruct the eighteenth of November as a comedy quite like him, and hardly anyone can resist laughing. Not even Karna. And then he sits in front of the fireplace, he crumples up paper, he adds twigs and wood shavings, he tells his stories and he lights the fire, pausing now and then to blow on the flames. He puts in Karna's logs, blows again, there's a faint crackle and he shares yet another strange tale from the eighteenth. Karna watches him as he blows and adds more wood, she leans forward, eyes fixed on the fire as it catches. It is only right that he lets all that sorrow burn.

2256

But sorrow still finds a way in. We can breathe a little easier here. Being in the eighteenth of November has become unremarkable now that there are so many of us. Several people have said so upon arriving: that you breathe differently the moment you step through the gate. Normality sets in. Together like this, there's nothing unusual about being trapped in a day. This is our world, and there is no need to keep explaining everything again and again.

But then, you start to breathe. Then, you begin to feel at home in the company of others. Then, this is what we are: people in a house. Not time-prisoners or loopers or repeaters or sporsettere or anything like that, just people. Then, you draw air into the sorrow, into the memory, into the loss, which comes to life and rises up and suddenly you feel it after all. What happened. Then, the easy breath and the simple life in our house only help a little. They merely breathe new life into all that is forgotten.

I think of the early days with Henry Dale. The feeling of having carried around a world you couldn't share with anyone. And all of a sudden having someone to share it with. To throw everything into a common pool. That is what we do. It is a world now shared. The house, the furniture. Bedspreads and clothes to sew. Rubbish to drive away, baking and pickling and preserving to do when new provisions are brought back.

It is a world full of practical chores. But in the midst of all this, amid the relief of not being alone in the eighteenth, amid the ordinariness and the daily routines: sprouts in need of watering, a new cauliflower recipe, cardboard boxes to break down, the crinkling of a bag, a friendly chat on the stairs, in the midst of all this, there is still the sorrow, which perhaps resembles Karna's all-consuming grief. At least a little.

You remember how it was. The future that vanished. How everything you envisioned came to nothing. The loneliness, the disquiet, the doubt. All of it in the distance now that everything is shared. Everything you went through. And then you understand that you managed to keep your head above water only through immense effort. That your feet couldn't touch the bottom: you simply had to keep swimming, no land in sight. Or that you were adrift in a boat with no rudder or sail, that you were lying in your white hospital bed, with no cord to pull if you needed help, no one to answer the phone at emergency dispatch, and if someone finally were to pick up: no ambulances, no driver to drive the ambulance, no petrol or electricity, no nineteenth of November. Day after day.

But then you look up. Then, you glance around the house. Then, you remember how each of them appeared. That there was Henry Dale in the eighteenth, there was Olga, and Ralf with his hopes for a better day, and now it is a better day, because we are many in the eighteenth of November.

It is not the same as a nineteenth of November. It is not a life with Thomas. It is not the same as getting everything back, because there, inside the relief, the busyness, the routines and all our discussions, sits the knowledge that the world is no longer the same. The sorrow that has been revived and flares up. The dizziness that has now passed. The understanding that has dawned. That you are no longer dizzy, that thankfully you were dizzy enough not to fully grasp how it was.

Maybe it was the gift of dizziness that Karna never got. All she got was sorrow. Maybe, at last, she is getting dizzy from chopping all that wood.

2313

We are many in the house. Heard all day long as Karna chops wood in the garden, the sewing machines hum along in the basement, a low thrum when you stand by the basement stairs or sit in the drawing room, and suddenly Karna has chopped her way to a woodpile in the shed and a basket of logs by the fireplace, and the machines in the basement have hummed their way to a shirt and a dress, and here by the window, where I've settled into a chair, I hear it all: always someone verbing their way to nouns, sewing their way to bedspreads and cushions, kneading their way to bread in the kitchen, slicing their way to salads and stews and November soups, folding their way to neat stacks of laundry to be distributed amongst the bedrooms, or now, as I write my way to filled sheets of paper in a chair, in a house. It doesn't happen often. We're far too busy, and there are already too many words in our day. We've rinsed our way to crispy sprouts, tended our way to potatoes in big pots on the windowsill, little tiny potatoes and tall, spindly stems that stretch towards the light, always something becoming something else, all these transformations, and still we get nowhere, we hustle and bustle, and the day stays the same. Nothing moves forwards. A storm in a teacup.

It is the sound of this storm that I hear in the house. The quietest storm, the gentlest confusion, an orchestra playing its way through the day, humming, chopping, kneading, writing, simmering, rinsing, tending.

I know: we are not an orchestra. We are a strange mosaic, a cascade of confusion, a jumble, a mess, a madhouse. We are a swarm of monsters, a bag full of hope. Is that what's happened? Has hope returned? I do not know. Are we letting hope into the house? Is it seeping in through the cracks? Hope in a teacup? Has it been living in the basement, behind all the things we've moved around? Was it clinging to the furniture? Has it followed us up into the rooms? Was it we who did this, shuffled hope about, scattered it through the rooms? Did we stitch hope into the bedspreads? Has it nestled in our hair? Are we hopeful? Or are we merely desperate captives of a day?

I do not know what we are. But we are here. Doors that open and close, voices in the hallway, pots and plates and knives, celeriac and leeks in the kitchen. I do not know whether you could say it's language that carries us along. Whether there is healing in sentences. We talk and talk. We hold meetings and have discussions. I do not know whether you could say that our meetings help us on our way. Whether we are getting anywhere. Whether we understand. Whether we are finding our feet in the eighteenth of November.

I think it may be something else. Maybe it's the hands. Maybe that's how we get our bearings. As if we understand the world with our hands, with our tools, as if we understand by working our way through this jumble, our meetings with all the objects: tool meetings, sandpaper meetings, our paintbrush meetings and pencil meetings, all our scissor meetings and needle meetings and the axe meetings with the firewood. I think it's our knife meetings with the vegetables, our mop meetings with the floors, our dishcloth meetings with the tables, our drill meetings with the walls and our screwdriver meetings with screws and rawlplugs, our grinder meetings with coffee beans and our tea towel meetings with plates and glasses. And now I hear car doors slamming, shoes in the hall, the groan of old hinges, hurried steps, people inside the house.

Suddenly I long for north, for snow. I long to sit in the lobby of a guest house, a blue lorry driving through the snow, boxes delivered to the kitchen door, I borrow books from a shelf where other guests have left theirs behind. I can walk in the snow, in all the whiteness, I can walk through the forest, to the churchyard and along the paths, I can walk around in a world of white and think that I am not dead, and at night it is silent. More silent than quiet. More silent than no sound at all.

But no one says I have to stay here. I know: being alone is always an option. There's no end to what one could be. One could be a ferry passenger. A cyclist or a motorist. A backpacker or a pedestrian. One could be a horse rider or a passenger on a plane. Or a pilot, if one wished. A deckhand on a ship. A kayaker. One could travel east or south or north or west.

One could go to Clairon. Of course, one can go to Clairon. Or to Ithaca, with Henry. Perhaps Olga wants to come to Düsseldorf, perhaps even further. To Naples with Mayte and the boys. To the Goldilocks house with Daniel. One could go to Poland with Anton and eat apple pancakes in a bay window overlooking the family's house. There's so much one could do. But one does not necessarily do it.

2446

We have held a meeting about the beginning and about forgetting. About our thoughts when it happened. Not what to call it, but how it felt. Because even if we can't find words that fit, we can talk about how it was. When time fell apart. Those earliest days of the anastrophe. We can talk without having found a word we can agree on. We can talk about the dizziness. About the sorrow, the maelstrom, the relief. About standing on the precipice. Staring into the implausible. A chasm. What we saw down there. What we did. What we thought.

It was the meeting's first topic: the beginning. Forgetting came afterwards. The suggestion came from Helena Ibart. No one knew who had put the slip that read *forgetting* into the cup – maybe it was one of the people who had already left – so we never found out what it was supposed to mean. But we stayed on the first topic for such a long time that we almost forgot the second one.

You can't hold a meeting about forgetting, Adriano insisted, you can only hold meetings about what you remember. You can hold meetings about anything, Sonia countered. She had hoped to hold a meeting about our bodies. How we treat them, and what they need. She wants to talk about our diet and our aches and pains. She wants to talk about small mishaps in the workshops, about sharp encounters with kitchen knives or cracked porcelain, about urinary tract infections and twisted ankles.

But first we would talk about our beginnings, even though many of us were already familiar with one another's stories and now retrieved the most condensed versions. I talked about burn marks and white bread, not in order to discuss the treatment of second-degree burns or simple carbohydrates, but simply because that's how it was: a walk through the rain with my burn, a slice of bread in the air, a gently drifting descent. There was the bag slung over the shoulder and the umbrella in the hand. I thought the fault could be corrected. I thought of warm jumpers and a house waiting at the end of my walk.

We listened as Henry D. spoke about his beginning, his lack of reaction. Or relief, almost. He spoke about vanished emails, about seven disposable razors which helped him keep count of the days, not just remove stubble. There was Olga making her way down the mountain, through the cold and the thawing snow. There was Ralf, at the casino, in a newly bought suit and expensive shoes, which he kicked off in the hallway before falling asleep fully clothed on the sofa. The shoes were gone the next morning, but he still had his clothes on. We spoke about Marlice and her gown-pilfering. The feel of the hospital gown against her skin, the well-worn fabric. How she wanted another one. It was cosy to sleep in, but where on earth does one go to buy old hospital gowns? And next thing she knew, there she was, stuck in the eighteenth.

And there was Rosi in the park. How she often thought of one particular moment just before she dropped the kids off at school. She came walking hand in hand with the youngest, a soft hand, she said, the eldest skipping ahead with a schoolbag on their back, an eager skip, with time to spare and oblivious to what was about to happen. She had thought about the moment time had come to a standstill. When did it happen, precisely? And what would have happened if she had been holding the little one's hand when time broke apart? Could you pull another person with you?

We heard about the extra days Anton got with his dad, and about the family dog, which he carried in his arms when it tired of walking. A glimmer of happiness crosses his face when he talks about time's halting: that it was also the halting of the illness, and that the dog is still alive, old and stiff-legged. It feels as if the halting is not without meaning, he says.

And Sonia's story, which always makes us touch our chins, gingerly, as if we had a wound that needed stitching, as if the anaesthetic hadn't quite set in. Peter's story, which we've heard only in fragments, because he would always rather talk about the day he met Sonia. Their beginning together. He remembers little of his own beginning, or he remembers it as a fog, because he drank so heavily at first that the days blurred together.

There was Chani Lydai and her life in Bremen. How she didn't want to go back to Konstanz, where she came from, even though her plans had been upended. She had thought it was her stubbornness that sent her into orbit in the eighteenth. Her refusal to just give up and go home.

There was Daniel, who had been travelling with a childhood friend. They had cycled all the way from Kent to the Mediterranean, but they'd had a silly falling out. A disagreement about where to go next escalated into an argument over how they made decisions. How his friend assumed that he knew best, that it was always his suggestions they ended up following, that he had grown used to Daniel letting him have his way. But not this time. Daniel had cycled off on his own. And then time had stopped.

Sarah Trent had been visiting a friend in Bern. She arrived on the eighteenth and spent the night at her friend's house, but when she woke up in her friend's guest room on the day she expected to be the nineteenth, it was the eighteenth again. She described her shock when she realised that neither her friend nor her boyfriend was struck by the breach in time. Her friend had been surprised to find her in the kitchen when she was supposed to be arriving later that afternoon, and her boyfriend had needed a lengthy summary of the events of the eighteenth of November before he believed she was telling the truth.

Afterwards, she split her time between her boyfriend and her friend. On the days she woke up at her friend's place, she would call her boyfriend in the morning to say that she had left for her friend's while he was still asleep because she wanted to get there early. He insisted that she should have woken him and not simply left. But when she stayed with her boyfriend and cancelled her visit to her friend, her friend was disappointed and accused her of sacrificing their friendship for her relationship. She felt she had let them both down. That she had somehow allowed herself to be carried off by the November day. It was as though the two of them blamed her for what had happened.

When she had got used to the thought, and since there was no help to be found, she had left, travelling for a while before checking into a hotel in Liguria, where she set about reading all the books she had been meaning to read. Long and short, old and new, and now and then she had returned, sometimes with a book for her boyfriend or her friend. Or with other gifts: a beautiful pine cone she had found beneath a tree, the most delicious lemons, delicacies she brought to Nyon, where she had lived with her boyfriend, or to Bern, where her friend lived. She still went back, though less and less often. Soon she would probably be off again. She wanted to bring her friend a jar of Olga's grape jam with crunchy seeds, if that was all right. But guilt, she said, that was what she felt. That she had betrayed them both and was enjoying life without them. Even now. By the hearth in the evening, with all of us, her new friends. In the conservatory, in the grey morning light. She found herself wondering whether she personally was to blame for time's halting. Whether it had happened because she had felt torn between her friend and her boyfriend. Whether it had happened because she wanted a break from both of them.

Many of us have felt as though we personally were to blame for time coming to a halt. That it was because of something we had said or done. Something we had forgotten or failed to do. A mistake we had made. A personal shortcoming or flaw. We are prepared to shoulder the blame for this mistake. And to try to put it right. At some point, at least, said Sarah.

I think I would correct the mistake immediately, if I could. Or most of the time I think I would. But I am fond of my friends here. Of Olga and all her scepticism. I am fond of Marlice, with her knowledge and many words. I am fond of Sarah, who knows what it is to watch the days pile up, blocking the path to the person you love, although she's better at clambering over her pile of days and returning. I am fond of Henry and Ralf. I think we would have been friends even if we hadn't met one another in the eighteenth of November's strange enclosure. Or at least, Henry and I might have been. I'm not sure I would have met Ralf or understood what he was talking about, had we met in life before the eighteenth. But I think I understand him better each day.

Norman Enser had been terrified when he realised what had happened to his day. Like something out of a horror film, he said. He remembered his second eighteenth of November as a day of terror. And the third. And fourth. It went on for a long time. He was on edge. As if someone were after him. He said that he was expecting to see a red dot on his clothes, someone aiming at him from a rooftop or window, someone with eyes on him. He began to scan the streets for signs of anyone tailing him when he went for a walk. A man he ran into twice in one day – could it be a coincidence? A woman, a little too absorbed in the contents of her bag until he had passed her. At first, he moved about in a state of constant vigilance. It lasted several days. He tried to flee, but the feeling fled with him. Eventually, it wore off. All of it. He came to understand that he was alone. That no one was after him. In fact, no one could remember having met him, even when he tried to make contact, and over time he began to feel that he was the one watching them. That everything was under control because he knew what they would do. When they would start rummaging in their bag. He discovered that he could disrupt their everyday routine – that he could pull the woman with the bag out of her pattern. All he had to do was clear his throat as he came up beside her, then she would stop digging through her bag and take a step aside.

It was a relief. He could live with a day that repeated. His fear and the thought of the red dot were worse than an endless stretch of eighteenths of November. Being under surveillance. It was worse than the thought of being wiped from other people's memories, he said. Better to be forgotten than to be watched too closely.

Narita Harding had been relieved from the start. She had dreaded the nineteenth, the day she was to testify at trial about the financial crimes committed by two of her bosses. She knew all the details, and on the nineteenth she would have to face them in court. Two bosses who had always been quick to respond, always certain of what was right and wrong. What she was doing well or less well. Who had told her that she too often forgot the information she was given. But it wasn't true. She remembered perfectly well, but they had given her contradictory information, and now she knew why: they had tried to confuse her. She didn't relish the thought of sitting across from them. She felt no desire to help clear things up. She had wished to remember as little as possible, and now that was coming true. She was forgetting. Initially, she had just wanted the whole thing to be over, but when the eighteenth repeated, she began thinking of the nineteenth as a day that had been cancelled and was no longer a concern. The eighteenth of November remained a problem, but it was a problem that had erased the nineteenth.

For Jeanne Fraizon, the halting of time was merely one in a slew of disasters. Her girlfriend had just left her, and one of her best friends had been diagnosed with terminal cancer. Jeanne and her girlfriend, Stephanie, had been planning to get married – they had already sent out invitations, even though the wedding wasn't until May. They had considered moving it to March, as Jeanne was worried her friend would be too ill to attend if they waited too long. But instead, the wedding had been called off. Stephanie had left her. Jeanne had been devastated. Her heart was broken, she was frightened for her friend, and time had fallen apart. All at once, she said. It was simply too much misfortune.

But just over four hundred days later, she had met Pia Karlevic. It had felt like a long time, but she could see that compared with many others it had happened rather quickly. Out of nowhere, on a perfectly ordinary evening, Pia had appeared. Another person caught in the eighteenth. And with her, love. The storm of misfortunes had abated. Jeanne believed it was misfortune's undertow that had dragged her out of time. Like in the sea. Once, she had gone swimming at a beach popular with surfers. She had stayed close to shore where the waves were very small, believing herself safe, but then a sudden wave had pulled her out towards the surfers. She called to one of them that she couldn't get back in, and he asked whether she couldn't get back in, and she said no, and she was dragged further still, out to more surfers, they were riding high on the wave while she was caught inside it, and she was swept seawards until another wave hit her and threw her back towards the beach. The surfers kept surfing, Jeanne found her footing and made it to shore, dizzy from being churned about and from all the water she had swallowed. Now, she said, she was no longer dizzy, just happy.

For Pia, the eighteenth had stolen in quietly. She had been on holiday and rented a house, a *gîte*, as she called it – in Burgundy, close to Nevers. It had been chilly. She had strolled along a nearby canal, watching the boats sail by. She had rented a bike for a few days, and one afternoon she had cycled past an old castle, complete with a moat and everything, though it appeared uninhabited. Large sections of the roof were new, but it looked as though no one had lived there for quite some time.

She had parked her bike and ventured into the castle grounds. A crane took flight as she approached. It was quiet inside the castle, save for the hum of a distant road, heard only when she stood by the tall windows. Part of the castle must have burned down and been rebuilt: some walls were blackened with soot and others had been repaired with newer stones. She had felt like staying. Several rooms still bore remnants of old wallpaper, and in one stood a grand bed with no mattress or base, but a faded canopy draped above. There was nothing creepy about the place, and on a whim she decided to stay the night. She had water and a packed lunch in her bag, as well as a warm jacket, and before long she had tracked down a couple of blankets in a room that might once have been a kitchen, with a cupboard still stocked with plates and glasses, as if the owners had made a habit of picnicking in their own castle.

Although it was November, and despite the recent rain, the rooms were neither damp nor cold. Pia spent the night at the castle, and left again the next morning. She slept a few hours, but for most of the night she had merely listened to the castle's sounds. That was all. But the next day, it was the eighteenth again.

Pia believed that it was her stolen night behind the thick castle walls that had carried her into the time capsule of the eighteenth. That time had simply stopped while she lay there listening. She didn't see the crane in the moat again.

Olga doesn't understand how anyone could believe that the halting of time is their own fault. As if the world were a place that remained stable so long as you did the right thing. A fragile balance you mustn't disturb. As if there were an instruction manual, and so long as you adhered to it, you could not be struck. By anything. And if you were, you must have done something wrong.

She didn't believe that. That is to say, of course she thought it made sense that she had ended up in the eighteenth. That she had a duty, a calling, a mission. That the world needed to be changed. That her anger, her worldview, her fundamental distrust of the system as such, somehow justified her entry into halted time. But not that she had done anything to send herself into our loop. She didn't believe that heartbreak or misfortune could stop time. Or that thievery and nights spent in deserted castles could be the explanation.

The world is not a calm sea where all you have to do is refrain from rocking the boat, she said. The world is a rocking boat, a ship in a storm, and when you're capsized, that's why. Because the world is a place that throws you overboard.

She believed our concerns about being at fault were an overestimation of our own abilities. As if we could set the universe in motion, out of commission, put the day on repeat. If we were serious, she couldn't see why we hadn't started putting our superpowers to better use by now. If it's actually possible to defy the laws of nature and the entire universe by stealing a hospital gown, then we'd better get to work.

You think that a single action can rock the world, that you have to hold such a delicate balance. But things can happen – and they do happen, she said. Or, rather, shit happens, she said. And sometimes really weird shit happens. Out of nowhere, your world shakes. But you're knocked down because the world was already shaking. Not because you rocked your little boat.

I don't know if it was the thought of the world as a ship in stormy seas that led Helena Ibart to speak. Normally, she doesn't say much. She is one of those people who needs coaxing to open up. She came here with the group from Liège, but she had wanted to stay, and after the very first meeting they attended, she moved in. She will sit in the drawing room for hours in the evening as everyone talks, some more than others, and then, as if prompted by something, she begins to speak. Most people turn to listen, and we sit quietly as she tells her story. It is not because she's reluctant to speak that she's often silent. She simply hesitates. Until she doesn't any more.

She began the account of her beginning as far back as the third of November, and we could tell it would take some time to get to the eighteenth. She started in Sydney, and those of us who had heard parts of the story before knew there was a long way to go, because we would be heading to Tasmania and sailing across the Bass Strait.

Helena had taken a gap year or two, travelling from Italy, where she lived, to Australia. She had visited friends in Sydney and set sail with them at the end of October. By November they had made it to Melbourne, and it was on their journey out of the bay that she brought us aboard. There was blustery wind and rainbows. Summer, yet not summer, she said. Dolphins and flocks of seabirds she didn't know the names of. Or rather, she came to know them because there was an ornithologist on board. After a few days, they had moored at King Island in the middle of the Bass Strait, where they were stranded for a few days, unable to continue due to strong winds. They caught iridescent fish and octopuses and gathered abalone from the rocky reefs.

Some days later, when the wind had eased off, they sailed out again – and this was the part she had been leading up to, because in the middle of the Bass Strait, after days of fierce winds, they suddenly found themselves beset with the strangest waves, which Helena couldn't help but tie to what happened later: the eighteenth of November and the halting of time. The waves around the boat had surged, not frothy whitecaps, but deep troughs and billowing crests that sent the boat soaring, she said, and both were equally horrific: sitting at the bottom as walls of water rose on all sides, and floating at the top, looking down into the depths. It didn't feel particularly dramatic, she said, just immense, but thinking of it now, she didn't like remembering herself back on the boat. She preferred picturing it all from above, like someone who had made it to shore, imagining herself out to sea, hovering above the boat. Like an albatross, she said.

It had begun in the late morning. The night before, Helena had stood a four-hour watch with one of the other crew members. There had been no immediate cause for concern. There were waves, they had worn harnesses as they always did when sailing at night. They had looked across the dark water; it had hardly rained at all, just a little spray from the sea. The waves were black and fairly large, but not enormous. But when she woke the next morning, they had sailed straight into the heaving swells.

She'd had to tell herself that it was perfectly normal, and no one else said otherwise – waves could be like this in these parts. One isn't in danger, even though it looks alarming, she told us, as if to explain why she hadn't been distressed. But then again, there was nowhere to go; she couldn't exactly hop off in the middle of the ocean. It was just the tail end of a storm, yet it soon became clear how fragile everything was: such a small boat and such big waves.

The next day, it felt like a dream. As if the mind refused to believe one had faced such gigantic waves and come through alive. And if one is alive, there's nothing to do but turn the memory into a dream. But it wasn't a dream, she said, waves really can be that gigantic. And now we followed Helena and the rest of the crew to Tasmania, and soon we were gliding down the River Tamar, the water calm, without a wave in sight, and when the boat had navigated safely down the river and docked in a small harbour, it was time for a celebration. They had disembarked and found their way to a nearby pub hosting some sort of early Christmas dinner, complete with turkey and Yorkshire pudding and chestnut stuffing and little chipolatas – Helena thought we should have all the details.

Already then, she had a sense that something had gone wrong, that the world had shifted: the impossibly big waves, a Christmas dinner that defied all rules of time and place, the upside-down seasons of the southern hemisphere. Everything seemed out of joint, and when she later left the boat with a couple of friends to travel around Tasmania, she felt knocked off course, as if she would never be the same again. Every crest had felt like the end, every trough like the final moment before the waves would surely engulf the boat. But it wasn't until she had safely made it to shore that this thought occurred to her. That was what was so puzzling: we seem to sail through life's crests and troughs, oblivious to what's going on. We go about our days, assuming we are safe.

She had never managed to shake the feeling, not even over the course of her many eighteenths of November. Jeanne nodded. She had been sitting right in front of Helena throughout the entire account, and many of us nodded along. Helena looked around, as if to make sure we were all still there. I wondered if maybe that is why she is so hesitant. She first needs to make sure that nothing will come crashing down if she begins to speak.

When the eighteenth arrived, she had already parted ways with her friends and checked into a hostel in Hobart. Her friends had returned to Sydney to work, but she wouldn't be going back to Italy until the beginning of the new year. Except the new year never came. She had travelled north to Brisbane and then to Darwin, but after a couple of hundred days in the eighteenth, she had gone home. And all the while, right up until now, she had associated the shift in time with the gigantic waves. Or swells, as she called them.

The way the residents of the house describe their early days in the eighteenth of November varies. Some include numerous details, focusing on the suspension of time itself. Some jump straight to the eighteenth, while others take their time, building up to it over many days – though few as slowly as Helena. You might find yourself wondering whether the pace couldn't be picked up, a niggling sense that there's something you should be doing. But of course, we know. Helena needs to lift the pieces into the room one by one, and there's nowhere else we need to be.

I do not know if it was because we had spoken so much about water, but suddenly I remembered the book about the history of drinking water I had left in the hotel room in Paris. I asked if anyone wanted to come with me to Paris. We could retrieve the books I had forgotten. But others, too, remembered things they had forgotten. Gita had forgotten that Yorkshire pudding existed. So had I. It was no great loss, but now several of us felt like celebrating Christmas. We began to discuss what ingredients our Christmas should include. There were many suggestions, and we would have to celebrate Christmas for days if everyone was to be satisfied, and then I forgot all about the books in Room 16 at the Hôtel du Lison.

2633

Our house has become a reception centre, a gathering place, a meeting point. People arrive alone or in small groups. Some arrive very quietly, as if they have slipped unseen through the back door. Others arrive like peacocks, strutting through the gate and up the driveway as if a red carpet had been rolled out all the way to the front door. Some leap into focus the moment we meet them, and within an hour, you feel like you know them. Others take longer to emerge from the background, a gradual reveal, and some you barely notice until suddenly they unfold – offering a story, an idea, a gesture, an experience – and all at once, you see them in colour, brightly lit.

They arrive with all their stories. With their explanations and patterns. With their sorrow and confusion. By bike or car, and some on foot. They come because they have spotted a poster or two, their curiosity piqued. But these days, more and more come after crossing paths with one of us – someone who has lived here or visited, and who mentioned the house and all our meetings. How you're always welcome at the meetings, even if you don't live here. We try to get to know everyone, but there are many of us, and often people are just passing through. Some move in and stay for good, others meet here, then find a place to rent together in town. Some only come for the meetings, others live nearby and make a point of regularly dropping in. There's a group in Lugano, there's Gita's group in Liège and Aikaterini Erb's group in Osnabrück.

One group has moved into one of the neighbouring houses, and others are eyeing a house a few streets away. They climbed over the wall and circled round to the back of the house. From the garden, they scoped out the rooms and found an open window. I think they're planning to make it their new home.

The pace has quickened. There's a cheerfulness in the bustle, in the days rushing past, in the comings and goings, and suddenly you realise that you've felt their absence while they were away, that one of their sentences has been buzzing in your mind, that you missed their particular manner of whisking a tray of glasses from the living room to the kitchen. A distinctive laugh. Most people return, not very often, but many still come to meetings, even when we are not discussing anything too important or solving major issues. I think it's the element of surprise they enjoy. How you never know what we'll end up discussing, how we let ourselves be guided by chance and little slips of paper. Sometimes the discussion ends after just a few hours, but there are always more to come. Accounts of people's journeys in the eighteenth: frightening or fascinating, critical incidents or moments of joy. And after two or three days, most continue on their way.

2896

She's here now, the woman in the yellow jacket. Her name is Vica Marls, though she wasn't wearing the jacket when she arrived. Still, there was something familiar about the group, Sonia said, even without the jacket, and despite the fact that there were eight of them – not five or six like the group she and Peter had caught sight of in Milan.

Peter and Sonia were repairing our bikes when the group appeared at the gate – or rather, they had just finished and were about to set off on an expedition to find fabric for bedspreads. At first, they had fixed up two of the bikes, only to realise that several of the others were low on air. They went ahead and pumped up the rest, and since Peter needed to go down to the basement anyway, he brought up a can of chain oil. After he had finished oiling the chains, Sonia insisted on adjusting the disc brakes on a few of the bikes, because she could hear a scraping noise when she spun the wheels, but after that, there was nothing left to fix: eleven roadworthy bicycles now stood lined up in front of the house, and they only needed two. Sonia had just returned the pump, oil and Allen keys to the basement, and they were about to head down the driveway when a group of people approached the gate. They didn't ring the intercom, since the gate was already open, but they paused there, looking up towards the house. Peter was sure that he recognised some of them and assumed they must have attended one of our meetings, but he couldn't remember when. He waved as if they were old acquaintances, but they hovered at the gate, looking a bit too bewildered. Sonia whispered to him that they must be newcomers and quickly motioned them inside. There were others in the house, she said, the door was open and they were welcome.

Not long after, when Peter and Sonia had mounted their bikes and were coasting through the suburban neighbourhoods, it occurred to them that the new arrivals might have been the same group they had seen in Milan. They couldn't agree on why they thought so, as there were no yellow jackets this time. Perhaps it was the scarf one of them had tied around their hair, or the upturned collar on someone else's coat, they weren't sure.

While we were having dinner, Peter and Sonia returned. They had been to a second-hand shop, where they had found some old tablecloths they thought we could turn into tea towels, and a few vitrified porcelain plates, but they hadn't made it as far as they had planned – curiosity had got the better of them and they had come home early. As it turned out, they were right: five of the newcomers had been in the cathedral square in Milan at a time that could fit with Peter and Sonia's visit. And, yes, Vica Marls had indeed been wearing a yellow jacket, though she had since left it behind somewhere down south. Finn Carell often wore his collar turned up, especially in autumn. It was probably this collar, perhaps paired with his hairstyle, that had reminded them of the group in front of the Duomo.

They usually came here during autumn, they told us. To Germany, or northern France, or the Netherlands. Of course, they then had to explain what they meant by autumn – after all, what else could it be? They said they travelled north when it was winter, and south when it was summer, or rather, when it would have been winter and summer, had the days still borne seasons. Olga laughed and told them about my failed attempts to create seasons, and I couldn't help smiling, as it was the first time I had met others who'd had the same impulse. There were plenty of people who longed for sunny days, and occasionally the odd person who missed the snow.

Several had also set off to find what they were looking for. But this longing for the months' slow, measured relay, each close on the heels of the next, the steady rhythm of the seasons – that, I had been alone in. At least, until now.

I told them about my encounter with the meteorologist in Copenhagen. How she had helped me find destinations and temperature graphs and snowfall tables. How I had told her I was scouting film locations. But I had been on my own, and I hadn't met anyone else along the way.

Vica Marls and Finn Carell had met after five or six hundred days. Their beginnings had been like most people's: confusion, uneasiness, then the joy of no longer being alone. Later they met Kira Merlon, who suggested that they go north with her in search of winter and snow. In Finland, they crossed paths with Stevan Karr, and Tia Ponsatty joined them in Milan a few days before Peter and Sonia saw them in the cathedral square. It must have been when they were heading north after their third summer, they reckoned. The first few times they sought out summer, they had travelled to Spain, but this time they made their way to Sicily, with Milan as a stopover on their way towards autumn.

Tia had been studying in Milan when the day came to a halt, and had mostly stayed in the city until she met the other four and left with them. No one had noticed Peter and Sonia at the café, even though Tia often sat in precisely the same spot they were occupying. Had she been alone, she probably would have picked up on the unexpected guests, but, she said, when you're part of a group, you don't pick up on all that much.

Sometime later, they had run into the last three of our new guests, Leon Batina and Mirs Darran, who already knew Sei Martel. They were the ones who had heard about the house in Bremen and suggested coming here, but they weren't sure we really existed until they were standing at our gate.

After dinner, Karna and I helped the new arrivals find mattresses and bedding. We made up beds for a couple of them in Henry's room since he had gone to Liège with Gita shortly after our last meeting, and two of them moved in with Rosi and Marlice in the flat above the garage. They didn't intend to stay long. They would be moving on, but they hoped to join us whenever our meeting days coincided with their autumn, Kira said as we prepared the house for their first night.

That evening, we gathered in the drawing room, and I was struck by an urge to travel north with them. If Henry had been here, I might have suggested we go together. Every so often, he has invited me to come with him to Norway, but that will have to wait until the next time they pass through, because he is in Liège, and I am not ready to leave.

I feel an odd sense of kinship with Kira and her group when they speak about their travels. I feel a longing for seasons. It doesn't surprise me that others have dreamt of seasons too – of snow and spring air, of summer evenings and mild autumn days – nor does it surprise me that they have travelled in search of those seasons. What is surprising is that they persist. That they can sustain the idea of seasons. As if these exist. That they don't eventually feel like simply embracing the eighteenth of November as it is.

But Kira couldn't understand it. That one might actually want to live in a stagnant day. In a house in Bremen, for instance. I told her that the days went by quickly. That they were not stagnant to us, and that we had grown fond of the grey light. That we grew sprouts, and now oranges and lemons too, in the conservatory. Could she smell it? A faint note of citrus in the mornings as you came downstairs, a sense of having drawn in a little summer, because after some time spent in the house, the buds had begun, ever so slowly, to open. And the potatoes had formed small tubers, which we had eaten. As if, together, we had managed to give time the tiniest push.

To me, the seasons hadn't felt true. Not in the long run. It was a big, cumbersome piece of machinery. Sometimes the whole thing rattled, and the illusion couldn't be maintained. But Kira didn't see that as a problem. Seasons, she believed, were always a little off. Even the real ones. You couldn't count on them to keep their promises. In fact, in her opinion, the seasons had never been as dependable as they were in the eighteenth of November. You could always adjust your position slightly, tweak your seasons and maybe next year you'd get closer to the mark.

But spring was hard to catch, I said. She agreed. On the other hand, it didn't last very long, she said. It's true, it wasn't easy to believe in spring when autumn leaves still hung on the trees. Winter was easier, you could always find a pine forest covered in snow somewhere. They had considered going to Australia for spring; there, the problem would be solved, because it really would be spring. Or to New Zealand. A few people they had travelled with had already gone. The first year, they had come back in search of winter, but no one had seen them since. Maybe they had found all the seasons they could ask for.

Four seasons in one day, noted Helena Ibart as we sat by the fireplace discussing it, and then she began to tell us about her days in Australia. Not about the ocean this time, but about what followed. She spoke of Melbourne's fickle weather, where if you wanted different seasons, you could get them – or at least a wide variety. Winds came from all directions: cool ones from Antarctica, warm ones from the north. She was convinced that in the southern hemisphere, it would be easy enough to cobble together a year of seasons. A believable spring. And summer, a proper summer. Winter in the mountains, if you wanted. She was sure of it. It was worth a shot, though Helena herself felt no desire to go. She was content in Bremen.

Right away, Ralf wanted to know whether anyone had plans to go to the southern hemisphere. He wanted data from new locations. I think that Kira and her group found us quite peculiar. A team who collected accidents and critical incidents. An assembly of people who had grown accustomed to eating rubbish. Who had furnished their home with the heaviest sofas of a bygone era and a faint smell of mothballs. Who had a sea of bicycles parked in front of the house and used cars only when absolutely necessary.

I think they are perplexed by our food, our clothes and all the things we've created together, the little pieces of life we've made fit. I see what they mean: suddenly you recognise a scrap of fabric from something you've worn day after day, a snippet of a dress you remember, all the stories we've carried with us, and then there they are, cut up, stitched and joined edge to edge in a bedspread or a cushion. I think they're baffled by how enmeshed we are, and by how spartanly we live in a world where you can have everything. None of them looked especially excited about Olga's grape jam with crunchy seeds, or the apple marmalade with lemon, which we served for breakfast. But that is what we have to offer. This morning, I was on my way to the basement to see if I could find something else for them. I thought there might still be a few jars of the apricot jam Olga made a long time ago. She has been saving them for special occasions, but I turned back before I reached the pantry. I don't think she considers fussy guests a special occasion.

2903

It's difficult to know whether we're still human. It was Sarah who had started having doubts. She laughed, but she meant it: she felt like something else. She didn't know what exactly – just something else. Not a human being. Not an animal. Not a ghost or a monster or some mythical creature, and then people began suggesting all sorts of things we might be if we were not human: witches and trolls, fairies and nymphs, cherubs, gods and goddesses, devils and vile beasts, miscreations, freaks, homunculi. There was also talk of aliens, cyborgs, clones, androids, that sort of thing, but Sarah said those weren't it either.

Sometimes, she missed human beings. Ordinary people, real people, normal people: her friend and her boyfriend, her family and colleagues. But still, she would rather be here. Be something else. With us. Most of the time, anyway.

She believes that something must have happened to us. That we have shed something along the way, that we've been infected by something, a virus, a kind of flu. Something that has wormed its way into our brains. The shock of time stopping, perhaps. Or a weather phenomenon that has altered us. A cloud cover, not rain or fog, just light clouds lingering overhead. A kind of transformation, stemming from within, or from without, or both.

You'd think we would have gone mad, gone to pieces, gone off the deep end, but instead something entirely different happened. An equilibrium of sorts set in. As if someone had brewed a healing potion and slipped it into our food, into our soups and gratins. A sense that there's no need to panic. Some sort of we'll-be-all-right tonic always close at hand. A feeling of calm. A resistance now gone.

Or maybe something has been sewn into the furniture, into our clothes. A docility. As if we ourselves had turned into woolly sofas, she said. Friendly chairs. Brightly coloured stools. But she didn't know why or how it had happened. Everyone laughed when she tried to explain, because Sarah's explanations are so long-winded that it's easier to understand her when she just stands there, waving her arms about.

She's always reading, maybe that's why. You get the impression that she sees the world through a different lens, as she wonders and speculates and unexpectedly breaks into bizarre reflections.

But she meant it, even though she laughed again, having abandoned any further attempt at explanation. That we are something else. Or that we've become something else. That we are on our way to becoming something else, perhaps. It's as if something had been stripped from us. Shaken off. Sanded down. Something had been washed away, or an insistent wind had stopped blowing. A sharp pain had eased.

I brought up my own feeling of having been rebuilt. I said it felt like a path had been cleared, snow shovelled aside. The reshuffling of the brain. Reconstructions. Something like that.

Adriano thought it was something else entirely. And simpler. That our arrested day had left us in an unusual position where we no longer had to constantly think about how to keep moving, whether we were lacking momentum, whether someone was in our way, whether we could keep up. A pressure had been lifted. The rat race and the hamster wheel and the career ladder and the competitiveness. That sort of thing.

And now? Who was pressuring us? No one. Where were we going? Nowhere. What was expected of us? Nothing. We weren't living in a world of collisions and obstacle courses; we weren't opponents or stepping stones or helpers or pawns in one another's games. There was no need to assert ourselves, perform, posture, pick up the pace, cross any finish line. We lacked for nothing, there was no need to fight for jobs or prestige or higher pay. We didn't need to flaunt our status or wealth with cars and mansions and gadgets or designer clothes, because anyone could have the same. If they wished to.

We had been alone for so long before we met one another. We had lost everything we had. Our futures and expectations. What was the rush? What did we expect? Not much. Even our discussions led nowhere, because who benefits from being right? Who were we trying to impress? One another? But why, when there was no harm in being wrong? Should we be afraid of one another, of saying something stupid? Should we worry about dirty looks? About someone rolling their eyes, giving us the cold shoulder, or whispering behind our backs? Should we be afraid to have strange opinions? But who doesn't believe strange things in such a strange world?

But are we human? And what are you if you're no longer human? This from Sarah, who wanted an answer, even though she knew she was asking the wrong question. How much of us is still human when life has become so sluggish, so suspended? And so easy, Marc began, but Karna cut in.

Maybe we're furniture, she said. Chests with many drawers. With intarsias and knobs carved from ebony and ivory and other plundered materials. Or maybe we're floors. Tiled floors, shiny and sleek. Or long wooden floorboards, without a single knot.

Then the conversation was flooded with suggestions, too many for any of us to follow. A rug, said Tona, who rarely spoke up. We were woven together, she thought, warp and weft. Colours alternating. Some bright, some muted. Light and dark. We lived here, or came to visit. We were reserved or outspoken. A rug made of threads, soft and woollen or coarse and wiry. But always woven together, a rug we could keep weaving. For a long time yet.

Or a bus stop, someone offered. Shelter from the rain. A

waiting room lined with benches. Wait here. But for what? We could be sliding doors, easy to push aside with a flick of the hand, constantly opening and closing. Or chimneys. Bouquets of flowers. Weathered columns in crumbling palaces. Caged parrots. I feel more like breadcrumbs, said Narita. Or flour. A material of sorts. Something that can be measured, but not counted. A heap of sawdust. Or liquids, said Marlice. A glass of water. A river. A rain shower. And on it went. For a long time, because once we begin, there's nothing to stop us.

But were we human before time ground to a halt? Maybe we haven't changed, maybe we were something else all along? It was Marc who suggested that we had been something else this whole time. Clowns, perhaps. Red noses. Or colourful balloons. Light and elusive. And now here we sit, wrung into shapes. Balloons twisted together to make a dog or a horse. A bird. Or a hat you can wear on your head.

I don't think Sarah believed we were getting anywhere, but she laughed and said we were all of the above, and suddenly Olga felt the urge to go outside, into the night. She suggested that, for once, we take a nocturnal stroll together. That in the dark you feel a little more like a human being. Some protested, because we were so warm and cosy in here. But Olga insisted, and now Anton did too, and before long several of us followed them into the night. It didn't make us feel more human or ordinary or normal, but there we were, wandering through the dark: little wonky columns, parrots, chimneys, chests of drawers, balloon animals, or whatever it was we had become.

2947

We're much too similar, Martine Paran remarked. We were gathered around the breakfast table. The house was full, as we had a meeting scheduled and were hosting overnight guests. She didn't really have time to explain what she meant because there were constantly guests to attend to and new people to greet. There was coffee to make, and several of the attendees had stopped by large supermarkets on their way and stocked up on items nearing their best-before dates.

Aikaterini Erb's group from Osnabrück had just arrived, lugging box after box into the kitchen, and Karel Varbek, who had called in at a brewery on his way from Liège, brought with him both a draft beer tap and several kegs just past their expiry date. It was not hard to guess that the day would be ending with a party.

Martine would have liked to elaborate on how similar she believed we were, and had put a paper slip into our cup, or rather, into our pile on the table. There are too many slips, so the cup just sits there, cracked, with the sestertius lying at the bottom. Often someone will insist on putting the slips in the cup, usually Rosi, but we always end up with a bag that we shake and shake until everyone is satisfied.

It was the practical topics that won the draw. That's usually the case, since there are more and more of them these days. This time, our meeting focused on the issuing of passports and identity cards, as it's become increasingly common for people to be stopped because their card is too worn or they no longer look like the person in their passport photo. It happens at airports and border crossings, at libraries and hospitals, anyplace where identification is required. Some thought we ought to contact the passport issuers in our respective home countries – not the official ones, as they would be much too slow, but those operating in the grey areas, where we might be able to pay our way out of the problem. Others felt this would be too much of a hassle, given that we come from far too many different places, and that it would be better to find one or more countries where we could quickly build good contacts. In that case, however, we would have to decide on a common nationality, and should we then learn the corresponding language? Should we organise language courses, and if so, when would they be held, and where? Before we got as far as debating whether our language courses should be week-long intensives or whether we should try to host them online, Ralf insisted, backed by several others, that it wasn't wise to rely on fraud and corruption. He warned it was a slippery slope and potentially dangerous, because wouldn't we risk getting into legal trouble with forged documents – and who here could claim to be an expert on handcuffs and prison cells? How would one get out? How could one get help if one was completely alone and unable to make contact with the rest of us?

He believed that the best course of action would be to accumulate information on the times and locations of IT outages or lapses in monitoring, that we had to find byways and round-about ways and practise diversionary tactics. He had encountered the issue at his own workplace, where he could no longer be sure his key card would work, but it came down to timing – arriving during the lunch break or when one of the managers was entering or leaving. If you greeted them on their way out or dropped a casual remark, there was a smaller chance of being stopped. That, he believed, was the solution: learning how not to get caught. Most agreed this was the way forward. It was a matter of information and timing, of finding open borders and narrow windows, and soon we had appointed a task force to handle the assignment.

The second topic of discussion was an account by Mirs Darran, who, after travelling with Kira's group, had given up her seasons and settled in Spain. She had met two people from a group none of us had heard of before. Reportedly, they had successfully grown a few types of vegetables, a fast-growing chicory and a variety of lettuce, she believed. It had begun when they moved to a depopulated area that had once supported large-scale vegetable production, but the climate had been too arid, the rain too infrequent, and eventually the villages, along with all the old greenhouses, had been abandoned. The group, numbering roughly eight or nine people, moved in and noticed that some self-sowed lettuce had begun to sprout. Most likely, the plants had bolted at some point and dropped their seeds – in any case, the result had been incontrovertible: fresh salad leaves in a deadlocked day.

We spent a long time discussing how such a thing could have happened, whether theirs was a day with rain, or whether they had to obtain water for cultivation, whether they had access to full reservoirs, and if so, whether there was a risk of draining them. We discussed temperatures and hours of sunshine, but since no one knew anything for certain, we let the subject rest and agreed to send out a delegation. Ralf volunteered, but wanted to wait a little, as he had things to wrap up at work. In the end, it was Mirs and Sarah who would go, accompanied by four or five others who volunteered later in the day. Ralf would eventually join them, and Olga might come with him.

As expected, the evening ended with a party, and it wasn't until yesterday morning that Martine returned to her point about how similar we were. She had given it some more thought during our meeting, she said, because it was plain to see: we were much too similar. It wasn't simply that we had all become chests of drawers or balloon hats, or a question of whether we were human any more. Rather, it was that we thought to discuss such things in the first place – not just Sarah, but all of us. That we spent our time holding meetings about the strangest topics, discussing language and grief and rescue operations and selves in cars as though it was the most natural thing in the world.

People are always alike in some small way, I suppose, said Narita Harding when Martine repeated her claim. There were only a few of us in the kitchen, and we were tired after the party. Most of the meeting's attendees had left by then, and once again there was plenty of space at the table. People were too tired to take in Martine's claim, but that didn't make it go away, and last night, when we were gathered in the drawing room, Olga brought it up again because she wanted to know what Martine meant. She had always seen us as rather different – we thought in different ways and wanted different things – but looking around, she could see it: we were quite similar. Though that was hardly surprising, given how long we had been living together in a suspended day. We walked about the house, living our far-too-simple lives, we copied one another, we mirrored and mimicked and listened, she said, even now. Look at us, sitting here, looking alike. The way we speak, how we're dressed.

But that wasn't what Martine meant, it was something else, perhaps something quite simple. She merely felt that most of us seemed to come from similar backgrounds. All of us in the house, those who had attended the meeting, and whoever else we had met. We were a fairly homogeneous segment of the population. A small subset of society. She meant both who we were and who we had become. Look at us, she said. No one old, no one poor, no one wealthy – or at least not before the eighteenth, when we all became rich, she said. Many of us are from Europe. Everyone speaks English or German, and maybe French. Several of us grew up in multilingual households. Many have a history of unfinished degrees, most have taken detours and side streets through life. Many held temporary jobs or were at a crossroads when the day halted. Few of us had children. Many were on the road or unsure what the future might bring. So, in a way, we were quite similar: doubters, people at a turning point or on a journey. People with loose-fitting identities and unsettled lives.

Maybe we were just the ones who had come loose, said Aikaterini Erb. She stayed behind after the meeting, even though the rest of her friends from Osnabrück had left in the afternoon. Aikaterini – or Trini, as she prefers – felt the need to elaborate. She imagined an autumn day, she said. Yellow leaves and a light breeze. Perhaps we were the loosest leaves on the tree. That was probably it. We had dangled from a branch before a sudden gust swept us away, whirling us through the air, alone or in small groups, until gradually we landed here and there, in corners, beneath hedges, in parks. Yellowed, brittle and perfectly still. And now here we were, rustling faintly in the wind.

Most people smiled at Trini's description, but few felt like dry leaves beneath a hedge. I said that I hadn't felt particularly loose – more rooted, if anything. Like one of the heavy sofas we had lugged up from the basement. I had wanted to stay where I was. I hadn't been in doubt or at a crossroads. My greatest uncertainty had been about whether T. & T. Selter should expand beyond books. Into scientific plates, for example. Or whether we should keep chickens. That sort of thing. I felt like I had ended up where I was meant to be.

Or maybe that was just what you thought, said Martine. Probably many of us did. Yet we've ended up here too. I couldn't really disagree, because I like being here, and I don't go anywhere, even if now and then I feel the pull to leave.

But I think it's true, Lenk added. He had been considering it during the meeting and the party, where he and Martine had manned the bar. He felt it was true enough. We were pretty similar. We have no chimney sweeps or stockbrokers, he said. No homeless people, retired housewives or refugees arriving by boat. We have no countesses, no old men playing pétanque beneath plane trees. No industrial fishermen or pet shop owners or animal feed producers. Where are the athletes: footballers and elite gymnasts? We have neither captains nor train drivers, we're missing binmen and seamstresses.

It had to be pure statistics and probability, Ralf suggested. Mere coincidence. Why would there be chimney sweeps here? How many of them are there in the world? What are the odds that a chimney sweep of all people would get stuck in the eighteenth? Or a stockbroker? And with that, another round of discussion was sparked, because several of us felt he had been too quick to jump to this conclusion. Statistics could hardly explain everything.

Some believed there was a whole other explanation. Maybe many others were caught in the eighteenth, but we had encountered only those who resembled us. Maybe we had overlooked the rest, maybe we didn't frequent the same places. Maybe they had simply slipped under the radar.

Or maybe not everyone roams around German train stations studying missing-person posters, said Chani. If you always travelled by plane or drove a car, how would you find out there was a houseful of people living in Bremen? While she hadn't come here after seeing one of our notices, many had. There was a notable concentration of young train passengers among us. Besides, she thought, you needed at least a modicum of hope even to respond to a poster like that. To go searching. Or to follow nighttime ramblers. Maybe we were the ones still clinging to the hope of an explanation, a solution, an escape?

Who knows where the others are? If they exist at all, that is, said Narita. Could some of us be dead or have gone missing without a trace? Do we know how many have lost their minds or gone to the dogs? Maybe they're locked up in psychiatric wards. Maybe they've simply given up trying to make sense of what happened. How many would we be if we looked closely? And why, she wondered, are there no eighty- or ninety-year-olds? Maybe we would have met more elderly people if we ourselves had been grey-haired.

But who says they're here at all? Chimney sweeps and stockbrokers and children and the elderly and the rest we haven't found? Perhaps it's just us. Perhaps we're the ones who never found our way out, said Daniel. We're the chumps who stopped in our tracks. Ever curious, always ready to ask questions and mull over the day's suspension – whether it was caused by something we did or didn't do, whether it was something we could put right. Perhaps our naivety was to blame for our getting caught. Who knows, maybe it's perfectly normal to be stuck in a day. Perhaps most people get out quickly, dismissing it as no more than a dream. We're the idiots who never made it to the exit. The ones who couldn't find their way home. It's fucking terrifying, said Olga. Maybe it's a test, said Jeanne. A really weird test. Or maybe it's a joke, said Marc, but this time no one laughed.

After pausing to reflect on the possibility that the halting of time had, in fact, happened to many others – and we were merely the ones lacking what Ralf termed return competencies – several people insisted we weren't so similar after all. It was the eighteenth that had blurred the differences.

Up close, we're just as different as everyone else, several people maintained. But Martine's observation still stands, said Henry. He had spent enough time in Liège to realise that it wasn't only here in Bremen that we were alike. The same applied to the other groups as well. Sure, we can spot differences, he said, but almost all of us belong to the Western middle class, of fairly ordinary European stock. The only real difference now was that we no longer needed to work for our food. Welcome to the leisure class, he quipped.

I said that he'd said that before. Once, back when we were a very small class of two. Or so we had thought. But I preferred the idea that we constituted a whole other class: the class of fools who ended up stuck in the eighteenth of November while everyone else got out in time. That normal people would have retracted their antennae, raised their swords, gone back to sleep, returned the wrong newspaper and demanded that someone get them the right one.

We were the timid, the featherweights. Maybe we were too polite to smash our way out of the eighteenth. We were the ones who knocked gently on the exit door and slunk away if no one answered. Those who did not kick doors down. The confused ones. Those who had forgotten their return ticket, dropped it somewhere along the way.

So now it's our own fault again, said Olga. We're the dunces, the failures, the meek, the weak. The patient suckers. Curious morons. Polite fools.

Pia Karlevic steered the discussion back on course. Did we feel similar? Were we, in fact, similar? She agreed with Martine: we were much too similar. Maybe our parents are more dissimilar, Pia suggested, and so we began talking about them, and while there were differences, they weren't particularly striking. Most of us had parents who could be described, in one way or another, as average middle-class Europeans or immigrants from other continents, well educated, often from large cities, neither wealthy nor poor. There were still no chimney sweeps or stockbrokers, though there were bricklayers and teachers, librarians and city managers, there were politicians and artists, a train driver and a lone upholsterer. There was Olga's father, who was a cook, and her mother, who'd had Olga young and worked in the hotel industry. When time came to a halt, Olga was living with her aunt, a teacher, and she had gone to a protest with her middle-class friends, and although she objected, Henry said she belonged to the perfectly ordinary middle class, just like the rest of us. There was Rosi's mother, a well-known psychologist, but whose own parents had been poor immigrants. There was Adriano's father, who was technically of noble lineage, though the family had never been especially wealthy. The sole relic of that past was an ostentatious chandelier in their living room, quite gaudy and totally out of keeping with the rest of his childhood home. Adriano didn't mind being called middle class, although he was probably at the poorer end of the spectrum. From there, we fell to discussing economic, cultural and educational class, which soon turned into a more theoretical debate – one that several people had clearly had before, Henry, Olga and Rosi in particular, but also Lenk and Martine, who often stayed up late in the drawing room talking while the rest of us slept. But little did it change: we were still quite similar.

Why don't we talk about our ancestors instead, Martine suddenly suggested, maybe then we'll become different. And so we did. Talk, that is. And become different. Or at least we branched out in so many directions we could hardly keep up, but it didn't matter, because the past began to sprout around us, plants that thrust every which way, climbing upwards, blossoming and bearing fruit, until we were surrounded by a strange forest, an untamed jungle, a meadow, a flowerbed where everything ran riot, an overgrown pergola from a bygone age.

It turned into the most peculiar evening. As we journeyed backwards through history, meeting one another's grandparents and great-grandparents, aunts and uncles and granduncles, it became clear that we weren't just entangled with one another, we were tangled up in one another's pasts. We had landed in the eighteenth together, we had sat, listening and talking, parroting one another, we had sewn and painted, built and repaired, pickled and simmered and baked, and perhaps we were much too similar, yet there we sat, tangled in one another's family lines: grandparents on opposing sides of war, some fallen, others returned, refugees and farmers and factory workers, criminals and victims, pickpockets and deported convicts, seamstresses and priests and sailors and housewives, jewellers and drapers, earls and milkmaids and serfs, midwives, revolutionaries, police officers, street sweepers, millers and shoe shiners, rice farmers and gardeners and weavers and governesses and suffragettes and civil servants trapped in bizarre hierarchies.

They all came to visit, filling the drawing room with their sounds: fishing cutters and steam engines and the jingle of the sheep's bells echoing up a mountainside, the wail of air-raid sirens and children's cries, the hum of market squares and sawmills, of combine harvesters, the clatter of pots and pans and the quiet rustle of pages in old libraries, and we no longer know if we are all different or much too alike, but whatever we are, we are it together, entangled in each other or grown together, too close to tell where one thing ends and another begins.

3112

We're a cheerful bunch inside a container of time. If time is a container, that is. We gather around the breakfast table in the conservatory, we convene in the drawing room as evening falls. People come and go, and the days race by, faster and faster.

A happy bunch, could one say that? I don't know. Can you be happy when you're missing someone? I dice onions and vegetables. If Karna Jeri is tired, I chop wood. I sit at the table in the conservatory. Olga walks in. A little later, Henry D. does too. He is heading out for supplies, so I do get out after all, because I tag along, and of course you can. Be happy. Can you be happy in a house full of friends? Yes, you can. Of course you can.

Can I be happy while Thomas goes about his house? Of course I can. It's not just me here. There are others to do the missing with. We wait. That's what people have always done. There has always been someone to miss. Think of that. Think of all the people who miss someone, and who go on living anyway. Day after day. It's manageable. Think of that. Of course you can be happy in the meantime. I unwrap and pickle and set out plates in the kitchen. Everything is easier when I rinse vegetables in a sink. When I chop and slice and think of the past. It's what people have always done when they missed someone. History helps. A little.

I don't know how you get used to these days, but somehow, you do. I think of other days. Days with Thomas. Days spent riding a bicycle. Days with wind or snow. I think of Romans, and of days with Henry on Wiesenweg. Conversations in the kitchen. Quiet evenings. Hours spent wandering through the city. I think of the sounds, of Olga and Ralf, of four office workers who step into a lift from different floors and stand there for a moment – no, for a long time, we are still here, and we are many more. Lift doors that open and close on every floor. Wrought-iron gates that swing open and shut. Front doors. People stepping through.

Tonight we discussed the topic of missing someone, and it made me start missing too. But perhaps it is the missing itself that I miss the most. It is the longing for Thomas, because that feeling is distant now, or perhaps it has assumed a different shape. I think of him going about the house, and how it's me he's waiting for. But then I remind myself that I saw him yesterday. The seventeenth. Why should I miss him already?

And I will see him again tomorrow. The nineteenth, I tell myself. It's soon. Tomorrow is soon, even though it may be many days away. If tomorrow comes at all. You never know if it will. Today is today, and the days blur together. Today bleeds into today. It's no disaster, just a day that has ground to a halt, and I know: Thomas is happy in his house, and he doesn't miss me, because I'll be back tomorrow.

That's how it is. I know: Thomas is happy without me, and I have known it all along. Without Tara, who turns up and tips a heap of days onto the floor in front of him and says: look at all that's come between us. Thomas is happy in his living room, and I am happy in mine. He is happy in his kitchen, and when he fetches leeks in the garden. Maybe he is happy in the rain. Soaking wet. A dark silhouette by the fence. I tell myself that he is happy, and that if I were to arrive with all my days in tow, he wouldn't be happy any more.

That is what I hadn't understood: he thinks of me, and I think of him, and both of us are happy. That is what I'm coming to realise now. It leaves me dizzy. A deeper vertigo. Alone. Leaning on no one. Or at least, not much.

3261

So you're at it again, swapping travel tales, Olga remarked. It is Kira's group that has returned, reporting back from a life in seasons, from the north and the south, and Olga listens, her expression sceptical, as they tell us about winter dishes and restaurants in the snow, about spring festivities and summer nights. Or perhaps it is concern on her face, because she can picture it: they are using up the world, laying it to waste wherever they go.

She calls them seasonal monsters, and it strikes a nerve. A bit, anyway – because I have been one myself, I have been a winter monster and a spring monster, I have been a summer monster, and I am still trying not to become an autumn monster.

Olga doesn't understand my longing for false seasons, she says, but I'm not sure that I do long for them. I think of winter in old Selter's garden. Flower heads bearded with frost. The leeks in the garden. The stubborn sage, its green tinged with blue. And the snow. Just a sprinkling. I don't need sharp icicles falling to the ground, I don't long for snowy roads that send cars skidding, hazardous skating rinks.

But yes, we do swap travel tales. We talk about coincidences. About the places we've all been. The guest house in the snow. They have visited it several times in winter. It's easy to find when you go north. Though now they have discovered a more secluded spot where the food is better. And the ski slopes, said Sei Martel. Excellent ski slopes.

Olga wanted to know if they had taken the resources into account. It wasn't a question she typically asked, but of course they had. Stevan Karr had done calculations that showed that, as long as they spread out enough, it would be quite some time before anyone even noticed their presence.

They had done the maths, they said, and put their travels into perspective. Into the bigger picture. And in the grand scheme of things, they weren't doing any harm. They were aware that they could lay waste to an area. They had noticed that they left traces behind in certain locations – but then they had moved on, sought new ground. It was about balance. Like on the ski slopes, it came down to small pivots, pinpoint shifts – adjusting precisely as needed.

Granted, they weren't living as austerely as we were here in the house, but there was only so much strain eight people – sometimes just seven, sometimes more – could exert on the world. After all, the planes still flew, or most of them did, anyway. The trains were running, the restaurants were open, the ships sailed, the menus listed food, and so they hopped from menu to menu. The changes came about all on their own. Each year, they strove to improve their seasons: to make the snow a little whiter, the meals a touch more refined.

And they spoke enthusiastically about the various places they had been – even a winter film I had watched while searching for ever more winter sounded more intriguing in their retelling of it. Kira and Sei Martel invited us to film nights with an October theme, because in their world, it is October – though they've gone off course, veering north far too early.

By their standards, it isn't Octobery enough in Bremen.

Kira said that she'd had a hard time finding October, that the light can be tricky to get right. I told her about the feeling of October in Clairon, a glimpse of sun, sudden spells when the rain let up. A wisp of October briefly rising from the forest floor. I spoke about looking for October in Düsseldorf, about sunshine in the yard, the days in my gilded cage, but I knew: all my seasons were November. The eighteenth of November, in colour.

Olga sees Kira's group as a swarm of locusts. They devour the world, and no sooner have they emptied a restaurant, café or shop than they demand more. I understand what she means, but I said that Kira struck me as a cheerful sort. That she made me think of October – not that I want October, but I do want to think of it. That I do not want to be a swarm of locusts, I would rather be a colony of beetles and woodlice and the wriggling worms in the compost. I would rather tend to what's been discarded than constantly seek new land to lay to waste. I would rather be here, I said, but I do enjoy their visits.

I don't know if they are seasonal monsters. Perhaps they are wishful monsters. They don't ask what's to be had. They ask themselves what they want, and then they go out and take it. They always want more: new places, summers that are better than the one before, exotic winter dishes, freshly picked mushrooms from faraway forests, they want fresh faces and travelling companions, they want brand-new shoes and plump berries. What's wrong with wishing for something, Stevan wanted to know, and what's wrong with getting what you wish for?

And now Sonia has got what she wished for, because Vica Marls has just arrived. She was wearing her yellow jacket, and not only that – she arrived lugging a heavy suitcase, and inside it was a jacket for Sonia, identical to Vica's and exactly the right size.

I spotted them a moment ago from my armchair in the drawing room. On the lawn, making their way to the little stream at the foot of the garden. I waved to them from the window as they passed by. They're out there now, shining brightly in their yellow jackets.

3346

We have held a meeting about our health. About teeth and vitamins and minerals. It was Sonia who put this slip into the cup, and it finally won the draw. Well, technically, she put it into the bag, because it is a bag, but we continue to say: we put a slip in the cup.

Sonia had written *health and sickness* on her slip, and so we spoke about our bodies, and about how we treat them, about hospitals and preventative measures. We discussed glasses, contact lenses and eye tests, first-aid courses, protein and vitamin D deficiency. It's not that we haven't talked about these things before, but this time it came up because Sonia's suggestion was chosen from the bag.

Sonia is our healthcare system. She has been from the start. She is our ambulance and nurse, she is our dietitian, and she was our physiotherapist until Norman Enser arrived and took over the role. She has administered antibiotics and stitched up wounds when someone got injured. She has dispensed chlamydia tests, treated eczema, tested for allergies and examined broken toes. She cures infections and tooth abscesses, though she always stresses that she isn't a dentist.

Some tasks she passes on to the hospital's emergency department, to a dentist or to Norman, who provides us with exercises and sound advice and a compression bandage if needed, and together they have started identifying clinics and specialists we can turn to in emergencies. That's where they're hoping we can help. As our group grows, so does their workload. Sometimes people travel long distances with their concerns, because they know there's often a doctor in the house.

Sonia was clearly surprised when her suggestion was drawn from the bag. There were lots of suggestions, and there were lots of people in the house, more than could fit in the conservatory, despite its enticing scent of lemon trees and flowers in full bloom. It's not just the buds opening one by one; small fruits are slowly beginning to form, and one of the larger lemons has started to yellow. It sits on the sill, and according to Chani, the fluctuating temperature by the window has helped bring out its colour.

So today's meeting was held in the largest of our living rooms. We had managed to find extra chairs, had laid out cushions and sat on rugs on the floor or on mattresses lining the walls, and during the breaks we squeezed into the conservatory, where thermoses, coffee cups and the pretzel sticks courtesy of Ralf were waiting for us.

Sonia spoke about the prevention of chronic illnesses, listing all the possible ailments that might still befall us, all the things we have not yet died from. She wants to teach us first aid and organise advanced courses for those interested. Hera Leng from Val Benoît signed up right away, as they're currently renovating the buildings there. They work on scaffolding, they cut glass, they weld and use compass saws, so injuries are not uncommon.

Sonia believes we must prepare for every eventuality. We need to familiarise ourselves with the healthcare systems and practise responses in the event of a crisis. She'd dealt with the system herself, she said. It's not easy when everything must happen within the same day. While it's possible to pay for prompt treatment in some places, she felt it was time to explore all available options. To build a network, create disaster preparedness plans and identify who can treat us if necessary, wherever we live. In Osnabrück and Liège and Lugano. In Bremen, when she is away from the house. In Lyon, where there is now a group as well. We can't afford to be caught off guard, not knowing where to turn.

We're not getting any younger, she said. Or healthier. We are many, our numbers are growing. Ideally, we would train more doctors. She proposed that we take a closer look at medical school curricula. Maybe it would be possible to piece together a complete degree by moving from one university to another.

She spoke of the future, and it was clear enough. She sees us getting older. She sees us growing old in the eighteenth. It is evident when she speaks. Her visions of the future: our numbers increasing, us aging and one day needing care. But then we returned to the practicalities – to the courses and first-aid kits and medicine cabinets and shift schedules and delegation of tasks. Still, several of us couldn't help but wonder. No one raised it at the meeting, but during the breaks in the conservatory, with the scent of citrus in the air and coffee cups in our hands, a few people remarked on it. How could she think we would be trapped in the eighteenth forever? Is that what she wants? How could she imagine such a thing: a life spent in the eighteenth, from now until we're old. Does she picture us living in this house? In all the houses nearby? A bunch of grey-haired fogeys with wrinkles and stiff joints and lifestyle diseases, with shaky hands and morning aerobics? Where does she get these visions? Or are they wishes? Where does she get these wishes?

Ralf nodded in approval at all of Sonia's suggestions. Or the practical ones, at least. I don't think he was paying attention when she spoke about the future. When she implied we might be the ones needing help. He sees it as a collective issue, and when Ralf says collective, he isn't thinking of us. He is thinking of all the people we ought to be helping. That, to him, is the reason we need first aid. His own project has stalled somewhat, but there are many roads to progress. In fact, he suggested that we integrate some reflections on the BeDaZy project into our health discussions. Perhaps we should drop the other topic we'd picked and take his project seriously. After all, there was a world out there in need of rescuing.

Now Milly Arcmole stood up. She agreed with Ralf about dropping the next topic. Not because she thought we should get into a drawn-out debate about his project, but because she had something of her own to say. And it was not intended as a criticism of Ralf's work. She simply wanted to emphasise that we were the vulnerable ones here. The mortal ones. And the lethal ones. Mortal and lethally dangerous. Because while all the people Ralf wanted to save did, in fact, wake up alive the next day, there was no reason to assume the same would be true for us. We're the ones who can die in the eighteenth. We're the ones who grow old in the eighteenth. Fall ill in the eighteenth. And, she said, we're the ones who can kill in the eighteenth, not them. When they kill, their actions vanish overnight. When we kill, we end lives. Irrevocably.

She believed that Sonia's project should be given first priority, and she couldn't understand why it had taken so long to arrange a meeting on the subject. Or why Ralf had inserted his own project into the discussion. But she just wanted to say – and she had her reasons for not mentioning it sooner – that she had been in danger, she had been ill, and she had killed someone.

It had happened on her day # 749, while she was still alone. It had been an accident. She had been driving, the victim was a cyclist, and it had not been the cyclist's fault. In truth, it hadn't been hers either, because she had felt unwell. Quite suddenly. It was evening, and she had been driving down a country road in Germany. In Brandenburg, she said. Darkness had fallen, the cyclist hadn't had any lights on, though that wasn't the cause, since she had spotted the cyclist before the collision. She had suddenly taken ill and must have fainted, because when she came to, she found that she had crashed into a tree on the roadside, or rather, first into the cyclist, then into the tree. She might have tried to swerve, but she couldn't remember anything. She didn't have a working phone, there was nothing she could do. Luckily, a car passed by moments later. An ambulance was called, but the cyclist was already dead. And no, she said, for the record, the cyclist did not wake up in their bed the next morning. The car was wrecked, the cyclist was taken to hospital. Milly hadn't been injured, but since she had no memory of the accident, and her head and neck didn't feel right, she had been fitted with a neck brace and brought along in the ambulance.

I could tell that Sonia didn't believe this part of the story. She objected: you don't put a collar on someone who's been hurt and leave them sitting in an ambulance next to someone who's been killed. If there's a possibility someone has a cervical spine fracture, they shouldn't even be sitting upright. And you certainly don't allow someone who has just run a person over to ride in the same ambulance as the victim. Not even on a deserted road in Brandenburg.

Milly paused. That was how she remembered it, but the exact details weren't the point. She wanted to share this with us to underline just how precarious our situation was. She probably wouldn't have brought it up at all – or at least not right now – but if we assumed, as Sonia apparently did, that we were going to be here for a long time, we had to fit this into our view of things, she said: that we are fragile creatures who bring death and destruction.

In other words, not only were we monsters devouring our world, which she recognised was a serious concern for many of us, we were also monsters capable of ejecting people from time entirely. We were both more dangerous and more vulnerable than those who moved through the world believing that the eighteenth was simply a day between the seventeenth and the nineteenth, because no matter what happened to them, they would wake up to the eighteenth again. Provided they were not so unfortunate as to run into one of us. To be hit by us, as it were.

And us? We would die. Without a doubt, we would die. Either slowly, after a long journey in the eighteenth of November, or quickly, in an instant, if we weren't careful. There would be no waking up the next morning. She was certain of that. We were in constant danger, and we were a constant danger to others. Ralf could think whatever he liked about our chances of building a better eighteenth of November. About our chances of rescuing those in danger in the eighteenth and helping them safely into the nineteenth. In principle, she agreed with him – his project was important, but as long as we didn't know whether the nineteenth would ever come, our work had to prioritise two things: not dying, and not killing. Right here. Right now. In the eighteenth.

She believed that the remainder of the meeting should be devoted first to Sonia's project, and then to finding ways of avoiding doing harm to others. BeDaZy would have to wait, and the second topic, whatever it was we'd pulled from the bag, would have to be cut.

Naturally, I offered to withdraw the suggestion at once, as it was my slip that had been pulled from the bag: fitting out a library on our first-floor landing. We had made sketches and drawn up plans, Daniel, Marlice and I, and recently Sarah had joined us. But it could wait. I had offered to collect some of the books from the house in Clairon-sous-Bois, not only because I sometimes missed the sound of old paper, the whisper of the turning pages, the scent of the past, but also because I believed that there were others who might enjoy those books presently gathering dust on shelves and in boxes in a house far away. Maybe also just a little bit because it gave me an excuse to return. To sneak into the house, sit for a while in the guest room listening to a person move about, maybe catch a glimpse of a silhouette down by the fence, a rain-soaked shadow. I could wake to the sounds of water pipes, to the patter of rain on the roof, creep into the office while Thomas was out, fill a bag with books, a suitcase perhaps, or two, knowing full well that I would have to head straight back home, to Bremen, to a house with friends inside. All of this I did not say. I said that the library could wait.

Milly's remarks sparked a lengthy discussion, for they set our entire future in motion. Many felt there were far too many unknowns and that it was high time we examined the workings of the day more carefully. That we needed to determine precisely how reliable the various observations of our recurring day were. Did people's experiences align, and if not, how significant were the discrepancies? Were Milly's descriptions accurate? Had she recalled events correctly, and what would the consequences be if she had?

Some people believed that we should adopt a systematic approach, launching investigations and drafting reports. Several proposed an immediate meeting dedicated solely to collating all our observations of the eighteenth's phenomena, along with all our explanations and theories, and Chani quickly volunteered to arrange the meeting at the conference centre where she used to work, and before the day was over, preparations were under way.

In the evening, after the last of the pretzel sticks had been eaten and we had polished off generous slices of aubergine-and-tomato tart, followed by a selection of sprouts – dressed in assorted marinades and vinaigrettes – and after much discussion about what we were already able to sprout and what we might one day grow, perhaps even tomatoes and aubergines, we settled in the living rooms, feeling full, somewhat agitated from the day's debates and a little uneasy about the prospect of the future. Some people had returned to their houses or hotels, others had retired to beds in different corners of the house, and others still huddled in small groups on mattresses and chairs, while a few had started kneading dough in preparation for breakfast.

I sat in the drawing room with several residents of the house and a few of our more recent arrivals: Trini and Finn, Marlice and Anton – and Milly, who had taken a seat beside Ralf. She wanted to make sure he didn't feel slighted or rejected, because, she assured him, she had nothing against his project.

She was keen to hear more, and Ralf was happy to share. However, he also wanted to tell her about the groups in the greenhouses he had visited with Mirs and Sarah. He had high hopes for both their vegetable production and their collection of critical incidents. Several of them had promised to collect incidents to report during his next visit, and he had started to think about going back, this time for a longer stay. Enchi Moll, one of the greenhouse residents with a background in IT development, might be able to help Ralf take his project to the next phase, particularly given his increasing difficulty accessing his workplace – especially the department with the most expensive and advanced computers. In any case, he'd had to call for assistance numerous times, and every so often one of the guards would eye him with suspicion. Now he was thinking of sourcing the most essential equipment himself and partnering with his Spanish colleague.

Hera Leng was sitting with Sonia on one of the sofas, eager to discuss the organisation of the medical studies Sonia had proposed, and someone seated nearby suggested that it might be wise to focus on a few key specialties – geriatrics, for instance, as it was apparent from the way Sonia spoke that she believed this was the path we were on: the slow march into old age.

But then Sonia said that she was pregnant. That perhaps we should focus on paediatrics and obstetrics instead. That it was time to examine our access to birth centres and paediatricians. Because maybe a future with children awaited us. Peter gave her a look – just the slightest arch of one eyebrow. Not because he didn't know; clearly he did, but I imagine they had agreed to wait a little longer before sharing the news with the rest of us.

It had been planned. The child, that is. They had been trying to get pregnant for a long time. And this wasn't the first time that it had happened – that there had been two lines on the pregnancy test. But the other times, they had lost the pregnancy, as Sonia put it, and it had come to nothing.

The room had gone quiet. People had begun shushing one another, first those nearest to them, then those a little further away. I noticed a few of the visitors seated by the door whispering amongst themselves, until one of them stood up and left – probably to tell friends in another room, because soon after, people started filtering into the drawing room, as if by coincidence.

This time, she could feel it. Feel life. Like a tiny air bubble, or a little marshmallow moving inside her belly, she said. A fish, maybe. A faint ripple. They'd also had a scan done, and there was a baby. A perfectly normal baby, judging by the ultrasound. Peter told us that they'd had the scan a few days earlier. We thought they had simply gone out to do the shopping for the meeting. And they had, but they had also gone out because they had found a clinic a few hours' drive away that could offer a scan at short notice. So the shopping trip had covered up their secret. But now the secret was out.

The conversation was now awash in congratulations and well-wishes, soon overtaken by questions that grew increasingly technical as the evening wore on. Because how could it be possible? What timeline did an unborn human follow? Or a newborn? Sonia said that she didn't know. They simply wanted a child, she said, and she did her best to respond to the other questions, softly and calmly, though many proved impossible to answer.

It was late, but there was a lingering uneasiness in the room. I could tell from the look on Henry's face that the news had stirred up memories. That his own son had once been two blue lines and a marshmallow or a fish or just a little ripple. That in this moment, he felt the distance more keenly. The loss. The longing. But then he began to talk about helping to bring a child into the world. About being there at its arrival. He talked about breathing techniques and antenatal classes and all the preparations leading up to it. It was Peter he was talking to. But then he stopped. They could continue the conversation another time, he said, and just then Olga came over and sat down. She had been out walking and wanted to know what had happened – she could tell straight away that she had missed something.

We had grown tired. Most people had long since begun trickling back to their rooms. I too was feeling quite weary, though not enough to get up and return to my room, where guests were already sound asleep. Little by little, those of us who were still awake had congregated in the drawing room, and I sat looking out of the window – or rather, at the dark panes reflecting the room behind me: small clusters of people who were still awake.

And Tara, said Olga, she just sits staring into the darkness, thinking about libraries. I didn't know what to say, so I let her believe she was right. But I wasn't thinking about libraries. I was thinking about children.

3411

I cannot keep up with the days, they slip through my fingers, disappearing into a cloud of visitors and household chores. I cannot keep track of our numbers. How many are we? We count, and there are always a couple more than we thought.

We are depleting our surroundings. That is our problem – or it will be, in time. It is not the size of the houses or the number of mattresses; there are houses enough. There are hotels and flats, there are plenty of places for us to live, but we cannot source enough food nearing expiry. We have our sprouts and the small potatoes, but it isn't enough. We've made efforts to grow greens on the windowsills, but progress is slow, and several people have floated the idea of travelling south to grow vegetables, though the results have been unconvincing. So far, at least.

Now we've started dipping into the provisions we had saved for the future, for the nineteenth, if the nineteenth ever comes, and many are talking about leaving. Sonia and Peter have gone south. They need sunshine and light. And they need calm. But they're doing well. We keep in touch, especially Anton. He and Helena Ibart have visited them somewhere in Italy, and they returned with ripe tomatoes, aubergines, courgettes, lemons. That sort of thing. And several crates of cheese, which Helena and Anton purchased on their way back.

Gita K. and her group think that we should all come to Val Benoît. That we could fix up more of the buildings, use the place for our meetings. Or maybe even live there. Renovation work is progressing, and there will be plenty of space.

Another group is living by Lake Lugano. They have the weather on their side, a clement, sunny day, and many people find the thought of a warm November day in Lugano quite appealing. Olga and Rosi have visited, but they're not sure the area could cope with a larger group. Maybe, if we could grow our own vegetables, but that would require greenhouses and south-facing hillsides, and no one knows whether it would actually work.

For the time being, we have no choice but to procure supplies from outside, because many of us are not ready to leave Bremen. We have a meeting to prepare for, a meeting about the mechanics of time – or a conference, as it's being called, since it will take place at Chani's conference centre – and in the evenings, we gather in the drawing room to discuss time and all our deliberations, everything we thought when time suddenly fell apart, the countless explanations that most of us attempted. Alone, because there was no one to share it with, or we shared it with someone who forgot everything during the night.

But now, we are many who remember. We have grown accustomed to time in the eighteenth, yet we still recall the tumult of the beginning. I remember the days of investigation with Thomas, our search in every direction, our theses and counter-arguments, our dead ends and all the notes we compiled, our models and observations and concepts.

It's as if people's ideas are given new life when we air all our deliberations. Up come explanations of the strangest kind: scientific and philosophical, poetic and meteorological, psychological, physiological, obvious or obscure, simple or so convoluted they go in circles, dizzying carousels ending in contradictions or bare assertions which only the most generously inclined could accept.

These evenings are cheerful. We report on confusion and fact, on paradoxes and fleeting glimmers of insight. On settling for the thought that clarity might arrive someday, that the days would pass, and they did, the days passed, what had been strange became ordinary and shared, and our bewilderment retreated, lay dormant, but now it returns, rushing back into the conversation, into the room, which fills with theories and observations, with arguments and counter-arguments, with elaborate explanations and scattered thoughts, the conversations spill over, we wander into dead ends and shadowy corners, along eerily lit avenues, paths dotted with brightly coloured lights, winding park lanes, and we know: there is no guarantee that the eighteenth of November is a day that can be explained, but we are many who look forward to our meeting. We discuss, we speculate and often, someone will laugh.

3446

We have held a meeting about explanations and the mechanics of time. The meeting lasted two days, and included both plenary meetings and smaller group sessions. We have watched presentations and examined drawings and diagrams projected onto the large screen in the conference room, we have discussed various categories and models, and tonight we continued the discussion in the drawing room – reviewing our many theories, our efforts to locate the cracks, the places where the day has fallen apart, all our ideas about what happened on the seventeenth, on the eighteenth, whether there will be a nineteenth of November, all our failed attempts to find a passage, a door left ajar to a progressive time.

It was Chani who had arranged the venue. Lately, she has been appearing at work sporadically, to head off any complications which might arise in securing space at the centre. She'd had her hair cut to resemble the Chani her colleagues knew from before, and she wore new glasses too, so any change in her appearance could be attributed to these, and when her colleagues arrived at work, she explained that there had been a misunderstanding: she had received an enquiry about a conference some time ago, but the wires had somehow got crossed, the client had not responded until suddenly they did. Now they wanted their conference after all and were prepared to pay whatever it took to arrange this last-minute event. Everything else had already been taken care of – accommodation and catering were sorted. All they needed were the rooms.

Chani's efforts bore fruit. The breakout rooms were readied, and at eleven o'clock we all convened in the main conference hall. Participants had been arriving in Bremen over the preceding days, with many contributing to the preparations. The Bremen groups had organised sleeping arrangements and meals, Trini from the Osnabrück group had worked with Adriano to collate the meeting materials, and the remaining tasks had been distributed among the other groups.

At yesterday morning's opening session, many people seemed mildly apprehensive, and the majority were unsure of what to expect. They were used to smaller meetings, some groups held their own meetings and most who attended ours were used to our somewhat random discussions. But as the day went on, spirits lifted, participants engaged in lively debate in various breakout rooms, gathered for coffee breaks, then dispersed once more to continue their conversations, carried by a mild euphoria, a renewed enthusiasm.

I don't quite know what brought it about. Gita thought it was because, at long last, we had the opportunity to engage in something beyond our daily chores, our renovations and planning, provisioning and the whole social menagerie. Maybe, she said, we had finally received new nourishment for our minds, maybe we had been deficient in perspective and abstract thought. Our thirst for knowledge had gone unsated for far too long. That's how she felt, and perhaps she was right, because today people eagerly assembled in the main hall for the presentations, and one by one the groups shared their theories and explanations.

One group discussed the suspension of time as a product of the mind. Could our brains hold the explanation? Were we suffering from a neural defect or a lapse in consciousness? Was the halting of the eighteenth of November a form of hallucination, something that had developed locally within our brains, some kind of damage to our perception of reality, an errant November day lodged in our memory, a doubling upon doubling of the eighteenth of November?

Or was it the others whose consciousness was impaired – those who awoke each morning believing it was the eighteenth of November for the first time? Many had come to accept this explanation in the early days, and the group discussing it had to split into two, as they simply couldn't fit in a single room. Perhaps the fault lay not in our brains: perhaps the missing memories in everyone else were caused by a delete function activated during the night. A cognitive malfunction, a black hole that sucked all events of the eighteenth of November into oblivion, a crack in the night, a disappear switch.

This was the kind of proposal that circulated in many different forms, both the idea of a hallucination on our part and of a defect in those who didn't believe they were caught in the eighteenth. The counter-arguments were of course just as compelling as the theories, and came in just as many variations. After all, if our eighteenth of November was indeed a hallucination, why were our bodies also stuck? Moreover, there was no way to explain how we could collectively hallucinate or how our defective consciousnesses could produce delusions involving one another. Surely it wasn't possible to hallucinate the same people, the same sentences, the same movements. How could all this be pure fantasy?

And if it was the others who were mistaken – if we were the ones experiencing the world as it truly was, and they were the ones afflicted by some anomaly causing their brains to erase the memory of the eighteenth – then why were their bodies implicated in the deletion? How could biology be completely suspended such that their experiences, their actions, would leave no physical trace? How had this happened, and why had the defect emerged just as we became trapped in the eighteenth?

Other groups had explored different variations of the idea of multiple universes. Maybe we had gained entry to a multitude of eighteenths of November, a reality previously inaccessible that we had slipped into, only for the door to slam shut behind us.

Or maybe we had splintered in some way. Maybe we existed in another version elsewhere – in countless copies, perhaps. Were we living in infinite eighteenths of November simultaneously, yet aware only of the one we occupied? Could it be that we were frozen within a prism of possible eighteenths of November? Or had we already passed into the nineteenth of November without knowing it? Or perhaps the others had? Maybe everyone else – our friends, partners and families – had continued on through time, existing in versions nearly ten years older somewhere? Are we there too? Perhaps it is just a copy of us that remains here, left behind in the eighteenth?

Others considered the question of how it had all come about. How had we entered the eighteenth? Where was the entrance, and where was the exit, if one existed? Who received tickets for the trip? Anyone, or only us? Had many others been on an excursion? In the eighteenth of November? On other days? Was it something that happened to just anyone at all? A jaunt across a day? And had anyone returned?

One of the groups insisted that our journey in the eighteenth could happen to anyone. That scores of people had undergone it and subsequently forgotten, maybe not on the eighteenth, but on all manner of other dates. This prompted a lengthy discussion in the hall, as it raised the question of whether, for example, Chani's colleague at reception had already made the trip. Take Frauke, for instance, as she was called: if she had been stranded in a March day two years ago – by her count, that is – say, in the fourteenth of March, just to give an example, repeating it seven thousand times, growing older and older until she returned, however that might have happened, then there had to be a way back, a way by which one grew younger and younger. Everyone laughed at the Frauke hypothesis, and Adriano, who was chairing, had to pause the discussion and ask that we continue it later, on our own time, as we wouldn't be able to get through all the presentations otherwise. Besides, he noted, it wasn't polite to use someone who was only a few steps away from the conference hall as an example. Even if she couldn't hear us through the closed door.

Some of the theories were more obscure and fanciful than others, but they always garnered greater interest than one might have expected. Many were supported by diagrams and models and calculations, some were underpinned by philosophical systems or scientific articles, while others drew on fragments of ancient texts or references to poets and mystics.

Rosi and Marlice had looked into the idea of time's standing still as some sort of microburst that had swept through the eighteenth of November. Marlice believed this explanation conformed to certain Hellenistic ways of thinking that she had studied back at university. It was worth investigating further, she thought, but the group had not got very far with this, because they had been busy collecting examples. Pia Karlevic was convinced that the crane that had flown up from the castle moat in Nevers played a role in the suspension of time. She regarded the crane's wingbeat as an instance of Rosi's microburst, and during their presentation in the conference hall, a long list was shared of examples gleaned from our descriptions of the events of the eighteenth. The falling slice of bread at my breakfast at the Hôtel du Lison was among them.

Another group had researched a seismological theory suggesting that unusual tremors in the Earth's crust had occurred on our very first eighteenth of November. Nirmala Holst, who had been a postdoctoral fellow at a seismological institute in Japan, had observed some seismographic irregularities that could not readily be accounted for. In the early hours of the eighteenth of November, she had been reviewing data from the previous night and noticed a fluctuation indicating a fairly sizeable earthquake somewhere in the Pacific region. It had been a very short sequence, which Nirmala had printed out and set aside to discuss with her colleagues. However, there had been no further signs of irregularity, and when the eighteenth of November arrived again the next morning – for Nirmala Holst, not for her colleagues, of course – the tremors could not be detected. The measurements showed nothing, and either it had been an error or a unique incident occurring beyond the bounds of normal time. Nirmala had saved her printout – why, she did not know – but the next day, that sheet of paper was the only physical trace of the peculiarities, and she had never found an explanation.

Helena Ibart, whose memory of the swells in the Bass Strait was still vivid and indelible, had joined the group immediately, because although her experience had not occurred in the eighteenth, several people believed there could be a connection.

Along the way, many pointed out that our explorations lacked a theoretical foundation, that attempting to build hypotheses or explanations would be futile without a thorough understanding of past theories of time – from the Presocratic period to the twenty-first century. Should our foundation not be in place before we start indulging in fantasies? Others, however, believed it was precisely the temporal theories of the past that had fallen short, that the prevailing conception of time itself was fundamentally flawed, that we were merely engaging with white or predominantly white and predominantly Western male thought. What did our static or cyclical or spatial time have to do with theories grounded in temporal progression? What could we possibly hope to learn from them? Should we not sooner incorporate overlooked perceptions of time: prehistoric, mystical, non-Western or female reflections?

My own group wasn't yet at the stage where we could present our findings, as our task was to summarise and categorise the various theories. I had been reflecting on the many different theories of time that Thomas and I had investigated during our days together, and it struck me that, within that brief period, we had encountered such a remarkable range of perspectives – all varying in their degree of obscurity – that we ought to create an overview of the different branches and recurring themes. I had considered retrieving the long-since-hidden material in Clairon, but I had not found the time. Besides, most members of the group had promised to assist Daniel, who was responsible for dinner yesterday, so we had to leave early.

A discussion that arose several times during our presentations was the discussion concerning the purpose of the conference – what was the reason for holding it, really? Were we trying to understand time, or to escape our recurring day? Perhaps the two questions were connected, perhaps not. In any case, by the end of the meeting there was a broad consensus that we should continue our explorations, although a handful of participants disagreed. Could we not simply inhabit time as it was? We had done so before. We had lived in progressive time, aware that each day was new and unpredictable, in a world of constant change, with death looming, with summers suddenly over, with inaccurate weather forecasts. All of this we had tolerated and grown used to. Back then, how many of us had attended conferences and group meetings about the ins and outs of time? Not many. So couldn't we simply come to terms with living in an eighteenth of November that kept repeating?

Fortunately, the meeting was drawing to a close, and we agreed that follow-up sessions could be held on the issues we wished to explore further. Besides, Chani pointed out, Frauke had children to pick up from kindergarten, and before long, we left the conference centre in small groups, almost all of us feeling buoyed and enthusiastic, and most offering a friendly nod to Frauke at the reception on the way out.

There had been one sad incident that affected several of us late yesterday evening. We had been expecting Sonia and Peter to arrive. Many of us, perhaps, had been looking forward to seeing Sonia showing obvious signs that a baby was on the way: her rounded belly, her joy, a yellow jacket now too tight, or whatever else we might have imagined, since every so often we had received updates on her condition, and everything seemed to be progressing as it should.

But that sight is left to our imagination, because Sonia and Peter lost their baby. That was how Anton put it when he came to tell us. It was not a lost pregnancy. It was not a *miscarriage* or a *misbirth* or a *stillbirth* or a *deadborn child*, or any of the other terms people proposed when discussing it. It was a baby, Anton said. A small human being. That was how they wanted him to describe it to us. No one could explain why it had happened. There was simply a small human being who never made it into the eighteenth of November. One of us was gone, or so we had to assume, though there was no way of knowing if the child had existed on the brink of two timelines. There was nothing to be said except that it was the first life we had lost in our eighteenth of November. Or the second, Milly added, if we count those we've killed.

The lost baby was not spoken of much last night, as the news came so late that most people had already gone to bed. But today, there were several who felt it was something we needed to include in our explorations. That we needed to seek out theories to explain what happens to unborn children in the eighteenth.

It was late afternoon when we got back to the house. We had said goodbye to those who had trains to catch, but many of us gathered and continued discussing all the many explanations and presentations late into the night, until, one by one, people began to withdraw, exhausted yet strangely alert.

And now I have found a seat in the kitchen, the only room in the house without guests. There are people asleep on the sofas, some in sleeping bags by the windows in the drawing room or under the table in the conservatory. I have closed the kitchen door. I have sat down at the table with my papers, though the worktop is cluttered with stacks of plates and rows of glasses – for now I leave it, because there are many of us to do the tidying, and I know that my notes are not necessary, because there are many of us to do the remembering too. Records are being kept, minutes taken, material and archival copies already compiled, but still, I write. Not because I fear anything disappearing, and not because paper is my only confidant, my sole witness, for the house is full of witnesses.

But I write that we are many in the house. That there are people everywhere. That I am not alone, that we are more and more, and that we talk and talk. That we borrow from one another's ideas and gestures, sorrow and enthusiasm, imagination and abstraction, all the circles, lines and curious cross-connections of our minds. That we become entangled in one another, and though you might think you can see it, you scarcely know where one person ends and another begins.

Maybe that is why I write. Maybe it's my way of being alone. Maybe the page is my door out of the disarray. A means of finding a way through all the thoughts and voices that blur together. To sit alone with paper and a pen and know that there is nothing but Tara's hand moving gently across the page, gathering the voices and gestures into that motion, ideas and explanations, all that we share, that we are many, a community, a flock, an odd bunch, and yet: my hand moves simply with all that has seeped into my sentences, into my hand, and I write myself onto a narrow path, sentence by sentence, I make my way forwards, tiptoeing, so softly. Alone.

3592

Ralf has been locked out of his workplace. That is, it has happened several times before, on account of various technical issues – there's nothing new in that – and usually someone lets him in. This time, however, although his key card worked and his fingerprint successfully opened the doors, the security guard had been instructed to stop anyone from entering the department. Some units had been stolen, equipment was missing, a suspected case of cyber espionage, the police had been called, and everyone was required to work from home for the day. Ralf should have received the message already; he must have overlooked it.

Ralf knew perfectly well what had gone missing, because he had retrieved some necessary equipment, that is to say, he had boxed it up, claimed it required repair, and had been believed when he carried all of it to his car, insisting it needed to be sent off immediately and could not wait for the usual courier, and then he had shipped the equipment to the group in Spain – but that was a long time ago. The strange thing, he remarked, was that it had only now been discovered.

Ralf had been in the office the day before and was unsure whether he might have left any traces. His suspicion fell on a particular folder, as he had brought all his notes for the pilot version of the BeDaZy project with him that day – it was, in fact, nearly ready to be launched – but now his folder was gone.

Ralf believed that this folder had attracted his colleagues' attention. That he had forgotten it in the room from which the equipment had disappeared, that someone must have come across it, been puzzled by its contents, and then noticed that the equipment was missing. Sure enough, when Ralf called to enquire about the issue of the missing equipment, one of his colleagues mentioned the folder. Although no one had linked the folder to him, the police had seized it.

The next morning, Ralf made sure to go in early, and now the folder was back, sitting in the empty spot where the equipment had once stood. He quickly slipped it into his bag and left the office before his colleagues arrived, and now he has gone. But not just Ralf. Olga went with him. I don't know how long they plan to stay away, but they left today, and it feels as though it will be a long time before I see them again.

Last night, we sat in the drawing room wrapped in blankets and jumpers, as we hadn't lit the fire. It has become harder to get hold of firewood, and although we've tried to spread our orders across several suppliers, and have sometimes procured wood from far away, we still only light a fire on special occasions.

Ralf and Olga's departure should really count as a special occasion, but Olga insisted it was no such thing. However, late that evening, when Olga stood up and I assumed she was heading out for her usual nocturnal stroll, she asked me to accompany her, not into the night, but up to her room, where she pulled out her sleeping bag and handed it to me. I asked what I was supposed to do with a sleeping bag that might or might not smell of salt water and the Frisian Islands. That was my problem, she said. The sleeping bag was now mine to look after, and she and Ralf would pick up my telescope in Düsseldorf on their way south. She was looking forward to days with clear skies. And nights. She was sure she would see stars in the Spanish night sky.

So now I have a sleeping bag, but Olga is no longer here. I waved as they drove through the wrought-iron gate this morning, and when they turned onto the street, I went down to the gate and waved again. The car had already vanished, so I gave a little wave to the empty space.

I thought of the day Olga knocked on the window in Clairon-sous-Bois – how I had thought she was a bird. But she wasn't a bird. I had gained a friend in the eighteenth of November, and I had left Thomas in Clairon.

Now we are many in the eighteenth, and I walked back up to the house, and there were people inside: Henry and Marlice sat at the table in the conservatory, Daniel and Chani had baked rolls and given a bagful to Ralf and Olga to take with them. There were plenty of people, but still, it felt strange to wave goodbye. Fucking strange.

3637

But then suddenly he called. Thomas. I will write it again: Thomas called. Last night. That is to say, my phone rang, I answered, and the voice on the line belonged to Thomas, and although it took me a moment too long to recognise his voice, soon I was certain – it was him, and now I am sitting on the train bound for Clairon-sous-Bois, still not quite able to understand what's happened.

He said he knew something was wrong. With time. That was why he was calling. Really, he would have just waited until I returned. Until tomorrow, he said. But he had grown uneasy. He wanted to hear my voice. He said I sounded different. Not very. I told him the same, because he sounded different too. Not very, but enough for me to feel uncertain for a moment.

I do not know if I was shocked. Hearing his voice was so strange that I had to sit down on my bed because my legs had started shaking, but once seated, my body calmed. It was only my thoughts that scattered in all directions, trying to make sense of what had happened. As if my mind was turning over every possible explanation, sifting through an endless array of more or less plausible scenarios, all while I sat on my bed and tried to keep the conversation afloat.

It sounded as though he had spoken to someone. Thomas, whom I had not seen for eighteen or nineteen centia, had now, for reasons unknown, broken with his pattern and called me, even though one does not make sudden calls when stuck in one's pattern. But he did call, and perhaps not only me, because a little later he mentioned Philip and Marie. For a moment I thought he must have spoken to them, that something had happened, that they might have remembered my visit, but later it seemed that what he knew was something he had read, which made more sense, at least once I'd had time to think. He had gone into the guest room, he said. Something had seemed off, he had noticed an electric kettle in the corner and a box with some tins of food under the bed. There had been papers on the table by the window, notes to do with the eighteenth of November. He did not know what I was in the middle of writing, and he had not got very far in his reading before he felt the need to call. He wanted to make sure I was coming home tomorrow, the nineteenth. Or the eighteenth, he no longer knew; we could call tomorrow the eighteenth, he just wanted me to come home.

I said I would. I was too dazed to explain anything properly, and it would have been impossible to give him a coherent picture of the situation, so I merely said that everything was fine and promised I would be back soon. I could hear that I sounded confused, but he didn't sound particularly coherent either, and shortly afterwards I realised what it was he had read. At first I had been unsure, but once we ended the call and I was sitting on my bed without Thomas's voice in my ear, I remembered the details from my last day in Clairon: that I had said goodbye to Olga and returned to the guest room with my box of provisions, that I had packed my bag as if for a mission requiring emergency rations, that I had closed my bag and pushed the box with the rest of my supplies under the bed. I had tidied the room, and on the table I had left a stack of papers, a printout of my notes from the eighteenth of November. That is to say, it was just a copy, and it was only the notes covering the time until I left Düsseldorf, as I had taken the notes from the visit to Clairon with me. I remember placing a little pile of white paper on top, though I do not know why the notes needed hiding, since Thomas never broke his pattern and did not enter the guest room at any point in the day.

But he did. He broke his pattern, and he went into the guest room. I do not know how it happened. There must have been a variation. A breach, a crack, a nudge. Something had sent him into the guest room. He must have stumbled and veered off course. And then he must have found my notes. And read them. Or started to.

While I was speaking to Thomas, I had the thought that I should remember the word *stumble* for the next time we – that is, those of us in the house, by which I mean the house in Bremen – talked about finding words to describe the problem with time. Perhaps I should suggest it at our next meeting: that we simply refer to our incident as *the stumble*. But then it struck me that perhaps I myself had stumbled. Stumbled over a letter in the contacts on my phone. Maybe I had accidentally called Thomas earlier in the day. That would make sense, because I had made several calls – first to Marlice, who was in town and had suggested we meet, and later to Aikaterini, or Trini, rather, who is listed under T. Maybe that was why she hadn't called back, I thought. Maybe it was Thomas's phone that had received the call, and the only thing that had happened, the only stumble involved, was my call to Trini, that is, to Thomas. Though that didn't explain why he had stumbled out of his pattern and into the guest room, but maybe he had tried in vain to reach me and then called Philip and Marie to ask whether I had shown up.

I do not know how I managed to run through all these thoughts while still keeping a conversation going with Thomas, but I did, and only when the conversation ended did it dawn on me that I could not have called Thomas by accident, because I do not have his number on my phone. It had been stored in the old phone, but not the new one, which I got in Clairon a long time ago when I needed to call Henry. There had never been any need to save Thomas's number. I'd had no reason to call him, and besides, I know the number by heart because it's our company number, and he has had it for as long as I've known him.

Nor do I know whether I will ever again find myself in a discussion about what to call our stumbling, our rather wobbly fall into a repetition. When will I next talk with my friends in the house about the vocabulary of the eighteenth? I do not know whether I will ever return to Bremen, because it feels as though my world has been shaken once again by a tremor, and I do not know what is about to happen. I am lacking explanations. For the phone call and for Thomas's visit to the guest room, but right now all I know is that I am sitting on a train, that I am on my way to Clairon, and that I'll be changing trains in Cologne.

The conversation with Thomas didn't last very long. Not after I had listened to his somewhat muddled account and tried to offer my own vague, yet far too simple explanation – that something was wrong with time, and that I would be with him soon – while my thoughts had strayed every which way. After that, we had murmured a few words about looking forward to seeing each other and that sort of thing, and he asked when I would be home, but when he began talking about train departures from Paris, I once again found myself unsure of where he thought I was, so I evaded his question and ended the conversation.

I do not know if Thomas spent his evening reading my notes on the eighteenth, but I know that I paced about my room, feeling a strange unease. That I looked up train times and packed a bag, but for some reason – perhaps because I could not fully understand what had happened, and because I had been struck by a peculiar hope – I didn't mention anything to the others in the house. Because imagine if, in the midst of this confusion, I had stumbled upon a passage out of the eighteenth. And not least: imagine if it were only me. If I would have to leave my friends in the eighteenth while I returned alone. It was not a thought I wanted to entertain, and certainly not one I wished to share.

But when I awoke this morning, it was still the eighteenth. I woke up early. That is, I hadn't slept much and I was neither rested nor calm, just on my way, in turmoil, trying to find a dress in which to meet Thomas. But nothing felt right, and I ended up pulling on a skirt Sonia had once made using fabric from our collections of discarded shirts and dresses and blouses, various strips of colourful cloth sewn into a skirt that reached my knees. After pairing it with a shirt I had bought in a second-hand shop and topping it off with a big woolly jumper, I felt almost ready to step out into the morning.

In the kitchen I took a few slices of bread and packed them in my bag, as I wasn't hungry yet, but I probably would be before long. In the cupboard above the worktop stood the cracked cup with the sestertius from Philip Maurel's shop and a single slip with suggested topics for our next meeting. A slip that must have been placed there by someone who had forgotten all about our revised meeting structure. I tipped the coin out of the cup and tucked it into the front pocket of my bag, and at a quarter past six I knocked gently on Henry's door. He must already have been awake, because he opened it a few seconds later, looking confused as he glanced at my bag and the big jumper I don't wear very often.

I told him what had happened. That Thomas had called, and that I needed to find out why. I said *stumbled*: that Thomas must have stumbled in his pattern, that he knew the days were out of order, and that I had promised to return to Clairon.

We stood in the doorway for a few moments, speaking quietly so as not to wake the others. He wanted to know more, but I said I didn't know very much. He suggested that we go to the kitchen for a cup of coffee before I left, but I said I needed to get going. I asked him to say goodbye to the others and tell them I'd had to leave early. While we were speaking, he had put on his dressing gown. He asked me to wait a minute – he wanted to walk me out, at least. There was something we needed to discuss. But I was already on my way out the door, I said, all packed and ready to go. I stepped closer, and he did the same, and we parted with a clumsy hug in the doorway. He told me to call when I found out what had happened. I said I would. Then we just stood there.

When I got downstairs, I put on my shoes and borrowed a coat from the entrance hall, because the big jumper I was wearing wouldn't fit under my own jacket. I think the coat belongs to Anton Janas – a grey overcoat with chunky buttons, but Anton isn't currently in the house, he left shortly after Olga and Ralf, and I think he is in Poland.

Suddenly I paused, having remembered the rain in Clairon. I took my shoes off again, crept back up to my room, found a pair of ankle boots more suitable for the weather, as well as an umbrella tucked away at the very back of my wardrobe, then spotted Olga's sleeping bag rolled up in the corner and took that too before creeping back down the stairs, carrying the lot.

In the hall, I put on the boots, slipped the umbrella into my bag and rushed out the door. There was a chill in the air, and I buttoned up the coat with one hand as I made for the gate, the bag slung over my shoulder and Olga's sleeping bag in my hand.

There wasn't much traffic on the roads. I wanted to walk into town. To take my time. I passed a bus stop but kept going, because once I had left the house, I was in no hurry.

At the station I bought a cup of coffee and a ticket, and shortly afterwards I boarded the train to Cologne, and from there I will continue to Lille, to Clairon, to Thomas and perhaps to an explanation, as I still do not understand what has happened. I edged down the aisle with my coffee and baggage and found my seat by a window, and here I am now, sitting among my fellow passengers. It feels strange to be on a train, yet oddly familiar, almost like coming home: the well-known movements, the people with their bags, coats and scarves. I feel uneasy when I think of Thomas, and mournful when I think of my friends in the eighteenth, because I do not know when I'll see them again.

A short while ago, a conductor passed through. She paused by the carriage door for a moment, and a few of the passengers noticed her and began reaching for their tickets. First one person, seated closest to the door, then another, who copied the action: a glance at the conductor, then a hand into a bag, ticket pulled out, and several more followed suit, the same motion rippling down the carriage, and I did the same, pulled out my ticket, but as it turned out, it wasn't tickets she was after. Instead she walked through the carriage with a clicking sound – the conductor, or passenger counter, or whatever she was – clicking once for each person on a small instrument in her hand, *click, click, click,* all the way down the aisle, and then we sat there: a group, a flock, a gathering that had just been counted. We were units in the same set, grouped together by this clicking sound, a group that steadily grew until she reached the end of the carriage, or perhaps, one imagines, the end of the train.

I have a new subset to inhabit. A person on a train between Bremen and Cologne. That is what I am. Not a person trapped in the eighteenth of November, though I suppose I am still part of that set too, but now I am also of another kind, a passenger type. I am connected to all these people by the little clicks of an instrument, and outside the windows, as we pull into the next station, another kind waits, the platform type, and when they come aboard, they will become part of our set, and now someone stands up and leaves our category and joins those on the platform, alighting, boarding, all these sets to which one can belong, and now people are settling in as the train moves away from the platform and rolls through the countryside.

Who are we? Do we belong together? Do we share a direction? Do we have something in common? Are others on their way to reunite with a long-lost love? On their way to becoming a group of two, finally together after far too long apart? And is that what I am headed for?

I do not know, but now we're moving on. I watch the landscape outside the window, and it's growing a little darker out there, as if rain is on the way. It's getting darker in here too, and the light turns on in the carriage. I look out of the window. It is raining.